HORROR
AND
HUGE
EXPENSES

T0150510

DESIGN & LAYOUT Nikša Eršek
PUBLISHED BY Sandorf Passage
South Portland, Maine, United States
IMPRINT OF Sandorf
Severinska 30, Zagreb, Croatia
sandorfpassage.org
PRINTED BY Znanje, Zagreb
Originally published by Ghetaldus as *Užas i veliki troškovi*.

Sandorf Passage books are available to the
trade through Independent Publishers Group:
ipgbook.com | (800) 888-4741.

National and University Library Zagreb
Control Number: 001103369

Library of Congress Control Number:
2021934652

ISBN: 978-9-53351-325-6

Co-funded by the
Creative Europe Programme
of the European Union

The European Commission support for the
production of this publication does not constitute
an endorsement of the contents which reflects the
views only of the authors, and the Commission
cannot be held responsible for any use which may
be made of the information contained therein.

This Book is published with financial support by
the Republic of Croatia's Ministry of Culture and Media.

HORROR
AND
HUGE
EXPENSES
STORIES

ROBERT PERIŠIĆ

TRANSLATED BY WILL FIRTH

SAN-
DORF
PAS-
SAGE

SOUTH PORTLAND | MAINE

"Robert Perisic is a light bright with intelligence and twinkling with irony, flashing us the news that postwar Croatia not only endures but matters."—JONATHAN FRANZEN

"Robert Perisic depicts, with acerbic wit, a class of urban elites who are trying to reconcile their nineties rebellion with the reality of present-day Croatia.... The characters' snide remarks could easily sound cynical but the novel has a levity informed by the sense of social fluidity that comes with democracy."
—THE NEW YORKER

"This jivey—and I should say x-rated-story stays with us."
—ALAN CHEUSE, "All Things Considered" NPR

"Despite the serious themes, the novel is largely comic and in many ways falls into the same genre of satirical anti-war novels that includes *The Good Soldier Švejk* by Jaroslav Hašek and Kurt Vonnegut's *Slaughterhouse Five*. Perisic constructs a series of long and entertaining scenes full of quirky dialogue and rhythmic interior monologue."—THE TIMES LITERARY SUPPLEMENT

"*No-Signal Area* is a mind-blowing read—a story of crime and heroism in the real-life aftermath of an all-white race war, told with wisdom, sophistication, and passion."
—NELL ZINK, author of *Doxology*

"In *No-Signal Area* Perisic brilliantly captures the absurdity and chaos of a society in transition. A poetic punk ethos saturates the book—defiant, anarchic, exuberant, and ironic—perfect for a story about hustlers and workers and dreamers and mercenaries in post-war, post-truth Croatia."
—MIRIAM TOEWS, author of *Women Talking*

"A sharp, subversive novel of ideas that seems to reflect an era in which ideas themselves are bankrupt."
—KIRKUS REVIEWS (starred review)

"Impressively blending the absurd, dire, and comic, Perisic relates often tragic events, but his characters somehow manage to persevere. This clever, ambitious take on the influences of capitalism on Eastern Europe will be perfect for fans of Umberto Eco."
—PUBLISHERS WEEKLY

Note on the pronunciation of names

We have maintained the original spelling of proper nouns. The vowels are pronounced as in Italian. The consonants are pronounced as follows:

c = ts, as in *bits*
č = ch
ć = similar to č, like the t in *future*
dž = g, as in *general*
đ = similar to dž
j = y, as in y*ellow*
r = trilled as in Scottish; sometimes used as a vowel, e.g. "Krk," roughly "Kirk"
š = sh
ž = like the s in *pleasure*

Contents

A Wheel of Cheese

WHIZ.

Martina crouched down.

Booom!

Some way behind.

It was talked about regularly in those days: if you heard the *whiz* of a shell you threw yourself to the floor because it was coming your way; it could land on top of you, or far behind. It was best not to wait and see. But she was in clean new clothes. She always visited her hometown in her best. She didn't want to fling herself on the ground. It wasn't close after all, and she would have soiled everything. And with that rucksack on her back with the big wheel of cheese inside, she probably would have hurt herself.

She walked on like in a time-lapse movie. Through the black-out-empty streets. Dirty, she'd be able to move about freely, but she wasn't used to this yet. She thought quickly and walked quickly. A bit farther. No more whizzing or explosions. She was on her street, walked a little slower, as if she was safe now, and looked at things with different eyes. Everything seemed deserted. Everyone was hiding inside. Not that hiding had helped those who'd lived in the house she was going past. Its front door was missing. She hurried again, in a silent run.

At her house she rang and looked up in the darkness. Dark walls, whose color she knew. She felt she had to wait a long time. Someone was looking at her through the peephole.

"It's me-ee!"

The door opened.

"Mama," she said, a little out of breath.

"Are you okay?"

"Yes, fine... I ran a bit."

A hug. Pause.

"Why didn't you call?"

"I knew you'd say I shouldn't come."

Mother was always so sensible, but she'd taken account of that.

"Why have you come?"

"Because I'm crazy."

"You are!"

They climbed the stairs. They had one of those winding spiral staircases in the house. Like in a bar. Father was watching TV in the semidarkness. Or was he sleeping? Both of them were on sedatives for sure.

Mother raised her arms a little and then lowered them again. "She's come!"

Father got up. Movements, as if he was in control of the situation.

As if they hugged.

Martina sat down at the table.

"I thought you were at the coast."

"Presto, I'm not," she said, showing her travel-weariness.

"Didn't you say ten days ago that you were going to the coast, to Cres? With that Tomislav, who's *super*?"

Her mother imitated that slang. Was it normal for a university student to describe a young man as *super*? Was there no other word, she thought then. But all that mattered to Mother was that Martina go to the coast, with whomever. It was that kind of summer.

Martina rummaged through her bag.

Mother looked at Father.

"Okay, let her catch her breath now," her father said as if giving up on something that had wearied him.

There was a lull in the fighting.

"I've brought you something," Martina chirped, pulling the cheese out of her bag with both hands, like a surprise.

She was not at all in the habit of bringing food from Zagreb. Big and round, it almost looked like a cake. Something that would bond them.

"Shall we cut into it?" Martina asked enthusiastically.

"But there's an alarm," her mother demurred.

"Come on, just try a bit!"

Mother looked at Father.

He looked at them from below, as if he was somewhere else in his thoughts. Then he raised his eyes.

Booom! A crash. A near miss.

"Let's go down!"

They padded down the stairs. There were two old armchairs below. Martina and Mother should sit there now, and he'd go to his room, Father said. He sat alone in the room. He was afraid, terribly afraid. Dared not show it in front of his daughter.

The armchairs stood one alongside the other below the staircase like the seats of a car. They stared into the wall as if it was a windshield.

Silence. The flashlight in Mother's hand.

"Can I go get some juice?" Martina asked, suddenly feeling thirsty.

"No, you can't."

"Why not?"

She laughed in self-pity. Here she was a child again, she thought; not allowed to have any juice.

"You and your crazy ideas. That's why!"

They stared into the wall as if they were driving somewhere.

"Where is your. . . Tomislav?"

"At the coast."

"Come on, tell me what happened."

Her mother's voice had become patient, which made Martina feel burdened. How could she explain it?

"I think it was to do with the cheese."

"The cheese?" Mother turned toward her and illuminated her face. "What's up with you?"

"I bought the cheese ten days ago. I thought I should bring something to eat when we went camping, sort of, so there'd be some basics. *We* always took stuff."

"Always fresh, always local," her mother boasted, unable to suppress her memory and restrain her pride.

Slavonija was rich and fertile.

"I thought, what can I buy in Zagreb? So at the market I bought the cheese from a farmer," Martina said with a frown.

She thought she could tell her mother the truth, although she didn't usually do that because her mother tolerated neither the truth nor lies, only something in between. She never intentionally told her the truth, only in the heat of the moment. But they were sitting there in the dark in front of the wall.

"When we arrived, I asked on the first morning if we should cut into the cheese. I mean, I saw straightaway that no one else was carrying such a weight, and I wanted the cheese to be eaten, or at least whittled down. But they had other plans and looked at the cheese strangely, as if to say, 'You had *that* in your rucksack?' I mean, we traveled by car so I didn't carry it for a long time, I'm not stupid. But for some reason I couldn't get the cheese out of my head all that day. And the next day, I don't know, I didn't feel like being pushy. Besides, it would have been strange for me to start it all by myself. I mean, look at the size of it! Have you seen it? I really don't know why I bought it. I mean, I try to think of every detail, just like you... and then I overlook something so big!"

At that "just like you" her mother huffed, her patience worn thin, but Martina continued. "Everyone, everyone else had brought small things or nothing at all..."

"And then what?" her mother interrupted angrily.

"Nothing, nothing. You did ask! It's stupid. He insisted on socializing with everyone."

"Tomislav?"

"Yes, Tomislav. You've got a good memory."

"So he's not so *super*?"

"They've all known each other for ages, and they all got on my nerves. I thought, like, 'Have you come with me or with them?' but it was a bit late to say it. He seemed not to have even noticed something was wrong. He seemed not to have noticed the cheese. I don't know if he perhaps felt uncomfortable."

"Why should he feel uncomfortable because of the cheese?" her mother asked. "What sort of goof is that?"

"He's not... I don't know, it sucks the way things turned out."

She stared at the wall.

Then she added, "The third morning, one dork started chuckling, you know, when I said, 'We could cut into the cheese?' and I was already a bit nervous."

Martina laughed, thinking about it now.

"The damn cheese! And then I... I told Tomislav I was going."

"What did he say?" Mother asked.

"He sort of tried to stop me. When he said, 'I don't mind you being here,' that was when I decided to leave. I mean, that's when I finally decided. Before that I thought I might change my mind. Then he really wanted me to stay. I saw that he found it embarrassing because of the others, that it was like I was leaving him. I said to him, 'When I see you by the sea like this, I find you... scrawny.' It was a bit nasty of me, and I said to the others a bit more loudly, 'What do you think, is he too scrawny for me?' They laughed, perhaps at me too, but I didn't care. That day I caught the boat to Krk. Jelena sells paintings there."

Martina felt she could hear her own voice in that lull.

"The whole time on the boat I thought about what to do with the cheese." She heard her own voice and her mother's silence. "I looked into the sea and thought about throwing it overboard. But I didn't chuck it. Then I was walking along the road in the sun, it was a fair walk to Jelena's, and I was lugging the cheese on my back. It was weighing me down, and I thought, How long is this cheese going to dog me for? I left it by the side of the road and set off. But then I turned around after fifty yards and looked. There in the sun? It was a strange feeling: my cheese sitting by the side of the road. Then I went back for it and started carrying it again."

Martina laughed to herself and said, "I was at Jelena's for two days. No one bought any paintings. We left together. Then, back in Zagreb, I just stared at the TV for a few days. And so, Mama, can I go up and have some juice? I'm thirsty from the trip, seriously."

Martina's mother realized the story was over.

"No."

"You can see there's nothing more to tell."

"Off you go then, but be quick!"

ROBERT PERIŠIĆ

Martina went up with the flashlight. Her mother followed the light with her eyes and stared up at the shelves, right above where she was sitting. She could no longer see them but she knew: up there was the home bar, with shelves full of bottles. She had been sitting there all the time and didn't ever think the bottles could be dangerous. It wasn't a safe place at all because they could tip over and fall. She got up and pushed her armchair, and then Martina's, out of the range of the bottles, and then she heard a detonation. And another. She pushed the armchairs and yelled to Martina in the darkness.

"Come back down!"

Upstairs, Martina choked as she was drinking the juice. She remembered a scene.

It had been on TV, two days earlier. A small girl said she had been sitting with her grandmother and grandfather in front of the house. They always sat like that in front of the house in the sun, the girl said. Then she went inside to have some juice. She drank the juice in the house.

Just like I'm drinking here.

When she went out again, no one was there. Everything was *splattered* through the garden and on the fruit trees, the girl said.

"Come back down!"

Whiz.

Booom!

Her mother's shouting stopped in the deafening crash.

I'm that small girl.

She made for the staircase. Fragments of glass on the floor. Now it was quiet again. Silence. One step at a time. In the spiral down. She saw her mother.

She was in one piece.

But everything was strangely shifted. What had made the armchairs and her mother move like that?

Her mother was staring at her. She was alive, wasn't she?

"What's so funny?" her mother blurted.

Martina recounted the business with the juice. And how she thought. . . Because she drank juice like the little girl. Her mother watched her with savage eyes.

"I know it's not funny, but. . ." Martina shook her arms in front of her, apologizing, with a grimace that resembled crying, although it was laughter, from the belly.

Her mother looked at her defiantly. "Look, look!" she said, taking the flashlight from her daughter and shining it up at the bottles.

"I was sitting below the bottles! I was sitting below them all the time, and nothing happened to me!"

Now they both laughed, their voices echoing around the spiral staircase, then they both held their bellies and their laughter was spasmodic and lingering, as if they were calling for help.

It rang below all the glass. They couldn't stop. Explosions nearby. The vibrations made the bottles clink.

Father came out of his room.

"He's alive too," Mother said, pointing to him with tear-filled, laughing eyes, but she couldn't get any words out.

Martina nodded, she understood and caught her breath, but she couldn't stop howling with laughter.

Father looked at them.

"D-d-d, do you want to try the ch-cheese?" her mother stuttered before once again hooting and stomping her heels on the floor, but she couldn't anymore, she had to stop or she'd explode.

Father stared at them and looked at the walls. Everything was intact.

ROBERT PERIŠIĆ

Those Guys Are Cracked

WE SPENT HALF an hour breaking down the door of the garage. Heavy iron. In the end, one guy blew it open with a grenade. There was zilch inside. An empty garage. I walked about in the dust, then I saw that another door was open. Why didn't we go round the side of the garage? How stupid we were.

"How stupid we are," I said to Mladen.

"Who?" he asked.

"Look at the door there."

He went up to the door, walked out and in again, to assure himself.

"Fuck. But what do I care?" he said, winking at me and contorting his face into something like laughter.

He went to the guy who threw the grenade. He was standing by the road with another. We hadn't met them before. Mladen wanted to take them to see the door, show them the zinger.

"Fuck off," they told him.

They thought he was trying to suck up to them. But he stayed standing next to them.

They were looking down the road and commenting on something, and Mladen grinned like an idiot. We went to high school together. As soon as he saw me in uniform he clung to me like a burr. I didn't mind. You need someone you know, although he was never my first choice of company.

I sat down in an armchair someone had put in front of the garage. Now I saw what they were watching: a fellow came riding up on a horse. As the house across the road burned, the black horse raced away from the flames. The fellow made a good figure on the horse. It really was a sight to see: the rider and his charging black, sweat-gleaming steed in the blazing dusk.

Mladen came up to me and asked, "Did you see that character?"

"What do those two say?"

"Those guys are cracked."

"Are we staying here? What do they say?"

"Absolutely off the planet," he said, shaking his head.

"Did you ask them or not?"

"Hey, bro, take it easy. What are you scared of? Why are you so chicken?"

He cast a slick look at me as if to say, "You're getting on my nerves, bro." It seemed he'd become a bit of a mover and shaker. He walked away from me.

There were about a thousand of us in the town. Just us. Sometimes you heard screaming, as if they'd found somebody. When Mladen came back, he was excited.

"You know what? Some guy found a red Ferrari in a garage! Where did they get a Ferrari from, man?" He raised his eyes to the dark sky. "Jesus, where do they get a Ferrari from?"

He looked at me again, stunned, and laughed, shaking his head.

"They're totaling the Ferrari down in the center," he said.

"Where is the center?" I asked. Until then, I thought we were in the center.

"Hey, bro," he tittered and leaned on my shoulder.

ROBERT PERIŠIĆ

"What?" I said, pulling away.

He laughed, and his eyes glued to mine. I looked away and waited for him to get serious. I didn't know what he was laughing about.

"You're up for it, aren't you, hero?" he murmured.

"What?"

"You're so damn jittery."

I kept silent now, I didn't get what he was thinking. I remembered how he was always nervous when he had to answer questions up at the blackboard. He would unwind with others afterward in the toilet, smoking cheap cigarettes and inhaling the smell of piss. Even back then he had a little moustache and was out doing jobs with his old man. They were repairing things. All manner of machines stood around outside their house.

Now he was different, but the same. We knew each other. Maybe that's why he grinned at me? Maybe because he wasn't that Mladen anymore? I don't know, I had a mental block as I waited for all of that to pass. I was cool, I really was in control of myself. As if I was at the dentist's or having an operation, I didn't want to think about it, I didn't want to be afraid.

Then we went to the center, to the main street. Some guy was revving around in the Ferrari. He would zoom past every five minutes trying to hit everything in his path—chairs in front of a bar on the square, fences. Like, he rampaged around the park in the car. He was driving it to pieces, ruthlessly. Fucking hell, talk about an animal.

Mladen stared as if hypnotized. At one point he reached his hand out for the Ferrari like a sleepwalker.

There was beer by the bucketload. A store had been plundered. The crew showered itself with froth. I took a few cans and withdrew into a doorway. I found a crate and sat down.

Mladen stood by the road.

"Come and have a beer, you can see everything from here as well," I called.

But it seemed he didn't mean to talk to me anymore. He commented on something out loud, but I didn't see who he was talking to.

The Ferrari came now ever more madly. Like a charging bull. It circled at the intersection.

Some guy climbed up on top of a kiosk and let off a long burst of gunfire into the air.

Fires smoldered, and a horse appeared in the Ferrari's head-lights—the black horse with the rider. The motor droned and grunted, and the horse reared. Another burst of bullets tore the sky. The fellow on the horse almost fell off. He called out and the shooting stopped. Then the horseman fired at the Ferrari and the bullets punched into its metal.

I moved away and went deeper into the doorway. There I blundered into an apartment. I had no idea where I was. The gunfight continued outside. I couldn't see my finger in front of my nose, the power was off. I flicked my plastic lighter and went into the living room. I looked behind me once more. If the house was set on fire, it was only a few meters to the door. I threw myself onto the couch, listened to the occasional shots, and sipped the beer. I turned over onto my side and pissed on the floor.

In the morning, a clock on the wall in the corridor tore me from my sleep, the ball swung, and there came an insidious beating.

I grabbed my Kalashnikov and pumped a few dozen bullets into it.

It fell silent.

Mladen's old man came today to ask me how it happened. My folks received him as a respected guest. We switched off the TV and sat down at the table with coffee and brandy, and everything was dignified. Mladen's father sat like a man who could bear the burden of tragedy. My father kept glancing at me and saying that Mladen and I had been together till the last. My father, equal in status to Mladen's, to a degree. I watched the two of them; that's how I always imagined heroes.

While I spoke, my mom walked around touching various things—the cups, the pictures, the vase, the tablecloth, the ashtray—as if she was trying to fix something.

Mladen's fat old man with his dark moustache puffed out plumes of smoke. My old man blinked, and now I felt again that he had never been satisfied with me.

They weren't satisfied with the story.

They went out together, like allies.

Afterward my mother said in a whisper, although we were alone in the kitchen, "I arranged that you don't need to go today."

"What?" I said.

"There are others who can go, I arranged it," she said, smiling proudly.

The clock in the hall began to strike.

I took my haversack and got up. Her smile changed to a grimace. She caught hold of my arm at the door.

I turned around and hugged her mechanically. The ball was still beating. It swung. I let go of her and turned back toward the door.

"Where are you going?" she whined and started to cry with a contorted face.

"I'm going to take revenge!" I fumed as I stormed down the stairs.

"On who? The car that ran him over?" she yelled after me.

I blocked her out. My thoughts were elsewhere.

I went down the road calmly and upright as if I was walking in slow motion, and my movements were strangely sinuous and fraught. As if I was being filmed.

"I'm going to take revenge, that's where I'm going."

After about two hundred meters I stopped. I stopped and sat down on a low wall, with my weapon. I looked around. Everything was entirely the same, the same old scene. I looked at our building as if it was far away, as if it was propped up on the horizon. I could fire anywhere.

Say Hello to the Tsar

HE TOLD IT to the woman who asked him what he was doing there, a woman he barely knew, but they did recognize each other when they went outside for a cigarette and then stayed out on the terrace, leaning against the tall bar.

"So he was driving, my mother was with him, they had a crash, and she was killed. It wasn't his fault."

Now he remembered he already knew the scenes that would follow: her sympathetic face, then, "Oh! I'm sorry..." Then the grimace of uneasiness when she didn't know what to say next.

He just nodded and felt aloof from the scene, like an actor watching his own performance.

Those expressions of sympathy were disconcerting, but people still made them, with care, so as not to offend him or disrespect the customs, which is sometimes the same, because people thought he might be offended if the customs were not respected.

It all had to be played out.

"I didn't see it myself, I wasn't there," he said.

He got a bit carried away with talking now; things always had to be explained.

He grew up with that story, he said, because all of it happened before he learned to speak, and when he began to speak and ask questions the story was ready and waiting for him. He absorbed it like it had always been that way.

When he heard that the earth was round, that surprised him much more than the story that his father had been driving, that his mother was killed, and that it wasn't his father's fault but the truck's.

The truck driver's, to be exact.

But his grandmother, who brought him up, said, "It wasn't his fault but the truck's."

That was the only part of the story that was obscure and slightly mysterious for him.

As a child, he used to look at trucks with suspicion; any one of them could have been to blame. He didn't see his father after that—he went away—but it wasn't his fault. The trucks were to blame.

He was left to his grandmother and her sharp tongue.

Later, when he grew up and acquired a sense of irony, he had to laugh at himself in moments when he retold the story.

Because if he told it and wallowed in bathos, it would sound as if someone else was inadvertently making fun of him. That person could imagine trucks just like he did—as mystical embodiments of guilt that rumbled and spouted smoke.

And when someone tells a story like that in a sad tone through and through, sometimes a person is listening who can barely restrain their laughter (*The poor little fellow, he thinks the trucks are to blame*).

Then that person covers their eyes, while the laughter sticks in their throat, and they say, "Sorry, please forgive me, but—"

and it becomes terrible, both for the one who laughed and the one who told the tale.

Not only *could* that happen, but it *did* happen.

Therefore he *could not but* acquire a sense of irony, and therefore he told the woman on the terrace that, honestly, only after a person expressed remorse to him did he feel emptiness in the place where others expect there should be something.

But that is only a void where others expect there should be something.

And a void generally opens up possibilities.

He disagrees with others, or rather with the ideas of others, about what is *normal*, and that is unpleasant, that is a reminder.

Yet he could not feel remorse for the way things were now, nor for what had happened, because if he truly felt remorse he would mourn being the way he is, and there is no doubt that without *the first thing* he would be an entirely different person—which he did not wish at all—and, yes, he would definitely not say such strange things, albeit entirely true, and he would not have to carefully apologize for it.

Yes, several times during the conversation he carefully asked *if he was boring her, if it was strenuous for her to listen,* and the like, but she watched him with interest and an unusual calm for such circumstances, because most people, as he well knew, were quick to hide the anxiety on their faces, or if they were of the jovial sort they would simply be dissatisfied with his tale and interrupt him in one way or another.

And he understood all that perfectly well because, if he had experience with anything, it was with people protesting when an entirely different life was presented to them as normal.

He told her again that he knew the story ever since he could remember, so it *was* normal for him, because it all happened before he was able to think it could have been different.

He could have added that it was entirely different to the sadness he felt when his grandmother died, but he didn't want to mention that because it could easily bring him to the verge of tears.

It wasn't so important, but—who knows—maybe the woman even liked him a bit, or was at least on the way to liking him.

It really wasn't crucial because he didn't have any intentions in that regard, but he didn't want to fall apart in front of her by mentioning his grandmother.

Yes, the story was always a problem, but when she asked him what he was doing there, he concluded that it was because his father lived there, and he had come to see him, because he was ill.

"Oh, it doesn't matter," he broke off. "That's enough of my story. So, what are you doing here?"

She hesitated, as if contemplating whether to keep talking with him or not, but then she laughed as if she was cheered up by the reminder of what she was doing there. Whatever it was, he was grateful for it.

She gave a little laugh and said, "My story isn't like yours."

"I can see that."

"Nothing special, nothing big," she said with a smile.

Her smile moved to his face too, because smiles can spread with some stories, just as other facial expressions can spread with other stories.

He wanted to hear what it was about, she clearly saw it on his face, so she continued. "You see, this story might be insignificant to you, but. . . There's someone here in Crikvenica who I've come to see. His name is Tsar Edgar. He's been living in the town library for two years. He's a yellow-orange tomcat. Very agreeable, soft, affectionate, friendly, and because of him children visit the library a lot more than before. As well as some adults. You know, there are people who just can't get along with others—I think you know what I mean. They're lonely. For some people, seeing Edgar improves their day, they talk to him although he doesn't understand them. I don't think he understands words, but I believe he understands tones. Frequencies, vibrations, rhythm. There's no doubt he distinguishes a lot of smells, too. Every person smells different to him. He can sense anxiety and fear for sure. Perhaps he even knows how sadness smells, and happiness. When that is combined with the tone of a person's voice, he certainly understands a lot of things. I'm going to write about him. Rather, not just about him as him, but about it all, about a cat living in the library in this town, which I consider big. See?"

He envied her as she spoke. She was in touch with serenity, and that showed on her face; she had become truly beautiful telling him this.

For him, on the other hand, the little town was gloomy, despite the sunny day he had spent walking the length and breadth of it, procrastinating his visit (and feeling it would only be bad for him, and it already was).

Only now could he actually place the woman. Yes, she was writing something. They knew each other by sight, from Zagreb, where they moved in the same circles, but if he had met her in a Zagreb bar they probably would not have felt they really knew each other.

But when you meet a person you barely know in a foreign city, your insignificant acquaintance is augmented. It's a very relative thing, obviously. If they had met in New Zealand they would probably have embraced like old friends.

Here he told her those few things he rarely mentions.

"Maybe I should go and see Tsar Edgar, and talk with him a bit," he said.

"There certainly would be no major misunderstandings. Cats know everything about road accidents."

He was surprised that she tried to be witty.

"But the library's closed now. Try tomorrow."

"I think I'll be leaving this evening."

When he said that he realized how much of a hurry he was in to go.

She thought of saying to him: But you haven't done what you came here to do, have you?

Then she changed her mind. She didn't want to go into that; she hardly knew him at all.

As if he guessed what she thought, he added, "There are some stories you can't fix. They're finished. Everything afterward is superfluous. He was superfluous."

She didn't want to delve into that, so she continued. "Just so you know, seeing as you've heard half: there's drama in Edgar's story too. There are people who want to kick the cat out. They write anonymous letters to the mayor. They exert pressure and claim their rights are being infringed. Apparently they're a couple. You know, Edgar has a function. He has his uses, to put it brutally. But the higher race—that is, two two-legs—see him as an alien and want him chucked out."

He looked at her as if he was wondering if she considered her story equally as important as his.

Perhaps he at least expected her to tell him what she thought, although he had broken off his own story and although he had said, "That's enough of my story."

Was he still waiting for something?

He had come here for a reason, but it seemed not to matter.

"You know, maybe it's sometimes best to get out of the story," she suggested.

"You're right," he said. "That's exactly what I intend to do."

He got up.

"Drive carefully now," she admonished.

"It wasn't his fault but the truck's." He laughed. "Isn't that funny?"

"You said you'd get out of the story," she said.

"Of course. Of course!" he agreed almost cheerfully.

As he was leaving, he called out, "Say hello to the Tsar!"

She watched him through the glass wall as he walked away. From the way he walked he seemed quite sober.

He vanished from sight. She became absorbed in thought, and some remote images flashed through her mind. Maybe I've also fused with a zero, she thought.

But who was this man?

And really, what was his name?

She couldn't remember.

The Party Was Just Taking Off

BLANKA AND I hit it off from the word go, instinctively. It was mutual. She moved her things into my place and we didn't even talk about it—it had become so normal for us to be together.

And we've been going for three years now quite okay, except for small differences in taste, which is normal. You know: she wants to watch a detective series, and me a documentary; she wants to listen to techno, and me rock or blues. Or, on second thought: I'd rather not do anything. I'd rather have a timeout, if I could.

Yes, frankly, I've had a few too many techno evenings in the Aquarius, and if Blanka wasn't so cool and intelligent, if we didn't live together, and if I didn't ultimately intend to marry and have children with her, some time when this mess all around us is over—techno could take a leap, believe me.

At first I thought: right, it's all in my head, I have to try and switch into that mode, you know, reform. I mean, if it's okay for her it can be okay with me too. Like, it's a positive form of reflection. You have to get into the rhythm, the rhythm of techno, you have to get to know it from within, to accept it democratically.

That didn't work at first, but never mind.

I mean, fuck, there's a bar there as well, there's always something to do.

And so, night after night, I wait for the dawn.

That evening I ordered my fifth beer and offered to buy the bartender a drink. I saw that the guy is okay, quite tidy. He doesn't hop and bop at all.

The two of us are observers, old school. There was a time when you could be just an observer, a tired guy.

Only the bartender and I were left. Alone at the bar. I had been watching him for months. He grokked. I bet he worked at a proper bar once. But the sound throbbed like airplanes strafing a column of refugees, so we never got to talk.

He probably didn't hear that I offered him a drink.

When I ordered my sixth beer, I said again that he should get something for himself. He brought me my sixth beer but refused to let me buy him a drink. That is to say, he didn't refuse: he said nothing and returned to his corner, like a boxing trainer with a white towel and a bad fighter in the ring.

And I was probably that boxer, you know, with rotten footwork. I looked toward the stage: they were butterflying like the young Muhammad Ali, with arms in the air after being declared winner. Not a trace of tiredness. But not aggressive at all—most commendable.

I'm just groggy and listen to the counting in no-man's corner; me, a light heavyweight with battered ears, despised even by his own trainer, who doesn't speak to him. He's just waiting to throw in the towel. The match reeks of a setup, fuck it. Imagine the feeling when you're despised by the very man who ought to be on your side.

The bartender probably thought I was one of them, for sure. What else could and should he think when I hang around all the time and just occasionally hop when Blanka comes up panting and sweaty to plant a kiss on me, and I reach her a Red Bull and shout in her ear, "All cool. . . Yeah. . . Nope, we're not in a hurry to go anywhere!"

The guy thought a hundred percent I was one of them but that I probably had some other defect as well, since I wasn't dancing. Absolutely no footwork. He probably thought I was just enjoying the music. He must have figured: who knows, maybe there are people like that.

Or maybe it was simply clear that I was a wimp.

I'm ruminating too much, I thought. What do I care if the guy doesn't want a beer? One of the little Mexican ones. All the more for me.

I pull the slice of lemon out of the neck of the bottle and gnaw off the flesh. I leave the rind on my teeth like a mouth guard and stay there in the corner. Never mind, this too will pass.

It'll pass, man, as long as they don't all take off to Slovenia.

I'm scared of Slovenia. Ever since they've joined up with that Slovenian bunch, in that so called chill out, they take off to Slovenia regularly. Chill is fucking weird. But Blanka sometimes deejays those parties, I support her, and occasionally someone even pays her. All of it together ends up lasting the whole weekend. We arrive home at five on a Monday morning, and I get up at seven because I work. Yes, on top of all of that I also have a normal job.

And I constantly feel as if I'm at a turning point.

As if I'm constantly taking a turnoff, veering aside, reflecting on something, I put on my blinker, but I've no idea where I'm going, but I think to myself, like: hang in there, man, your whole life is ahead of you, now you're at a turning point, stand your ground.

So at seven every morning I drip Visine into my eyes because it refreshes the capillaries, then I shave and switch my psyche to work; I become somebody else, or somebody else again, I don't really know anymore how many of us there are. Then I wake

Blanka, but she simply can't get out of bed. It really would be a big thing for her to become a deejay.

Living like this, her jobs get cancelled. But I still support her, I pay for the apartment and drive the company's Golf, an old white diesel GTD, a bit of a box. It's nothing out of the ordinary, but it's good when we go to Slovenia. And we go, of course.

The GTD goes too. I mean, I can't be such a wimp as to turn in early while the rave goes on. I hear there will be a trove of beer and underground deejays in a private house. I go because of the beer and Blanka.

I'm young, man, I'm still young; I drink Rehydromix, I drink Red Bull and drive.

And so I did the long drive to that house up on a hill, overlooking Dobova, and there was snow, not slush, but real, untouched morning snow, and we crackled over it first, like astronauts on an expedition to found new techno colonies. Four cars in convoy. In the Golf: me, Blanka, and three deejays squeezed in the back. The knees of one of them jabbed into me, and in the rearview mirror I saw the white head of another, who had a long neck like a Gothic Madonna.

Two of the guys in the back were chatting and name-dropping with Blanka, while the deathly pale guy fell asleep. I drove and said, "What a beautiful landscape." Then I thought: Go on, go on, say something about the weather too.

We arrived.

I went in search of beer.

I sat down in the hall near the bathroom.

I saw the deathly pale fellow brushing his teeth. He had brought a toothbrush with him. That wasn't a good sign.

Then he took a roll of something out of his pocket like an enormous joint: a pair of cloth slippers.

Talk about a role model, I thought.

I drank beer.

The party was still just taking off.

I drank that beer and waited.

Time passed: doof-doof. Everything was cool. *Doof-doof.* I was still holding up. *Doof-doof.* Hey, I've got a job, and I go out partying. *Doof-doof.* And Blanka was here. *Doof-doof.* She made me younger. *Doof-doof.*

But there was something I didn't get.

At one point I called Blanka outside, in front of the door. She looked at me wide-eyed, as if it was something serious.

"Blanka, listen, there's a problem," I said.

"What?"

"They've bought alcohol-free beer," I explained.

"Hmm," she looked at me. She was a bit nervous and just couldn't stand still.

"I didn't even look what it says. I've drunk a few cans and I'm as sober as anything. Try and get off your high and let's scram."

Bobbing, probably so as to keep warm, she said, "But we told the guys we'd drive them back!"

"Yes, but they said they'd buy beer!"

I threw the can into the snow. Environmentally unsound, I know.

"Besides," I said, "they have toothbrushes, and they even brought slippers. They've got all they need for a long stay out in the wild."

"Pop a candy and you'll be okay!" she said. "Or just hold on a bit longer."

I waited.

Then I got bored, so I popped one.

I started to dance, although in a kind of ironic way. But a celebration began, and it seemed everyone was celebrating because of me—a baptism of fire, an induction, or were they perhaps just having me on? Blanka kissed me. I felt her tongue. She nibbled my lips. And it was the two of us again, instinctively. Soon we were making love in a side room. Rhythmically. But at one point I felt she was crying and I stopped.

"What's wrong?" I asked.

"I don't know," she said.

We lay on that mattress and I touched her hair.

"A sadness, but now it's gone," she breathed into my neck and snuggled up to me.

We got home on Monday at five.

"Wake me at seven thirty," she said.

"Okay, Blanka, but you won't want to get up."

"No, do whatever to wake me up!"

"I always wake you, but you never get up."

"No, seriously! I have a kid to mind over in Sopot."

"Got it."

"Seriously. It's a long-term arrangement. The kid can't stay alone, see? Throw me out of bed, whatever it takes."

She fell asleep, but I couldn't. It was too late to take a Valium. If I popped one now, it would all be even harder. I just lay on my side and stared from the pillow through the window, askance, like a dazed bird. I closed my eyes and counted to a hundred, slowed my breathing, relaxed my muscles, thought about pornography. I might have been half asleep when the alarm rang.

I shaved, got dressed, dripped some Visine into my eyes, took an aspirin, and made coffee. I did everything.

Then I went to her. "Blanka, time to wake up."

No reaction.

"Blanka, get up, stop messing around!"

Nothing.

"Blanka! Open your eyes and fucking well get up!" I yelled. "Hey, you've got a kid to look after in Sopot, you have an arrangement!"

ROBERT PERIŠIĆ

"Leave me alone," she muttered.

"Heeey, reveille! The kid! Sopot! Get up!" I screamed in her ear, shaking her.

She opened her eyes in fright, then groaned, "You're such a pain!" and closed them again.

I grabbed her by the legs and started pulling.

She kicked about, banging against the side of the bed.

She thrust her head into the pillow, clenched it, and whined, "Jesus, you idiot!"

And dragged herself back into bed.

Nothing for it: I grabbed her under both arms and hauled her to the bath. She cursed at me. Perhaps she even bashed into some things on the way. Then I turned on the shower.

"Let me go!" she growled through her clenched teeth.

I showered her, holding her by the neck, until she tore away and started to flail her arms at me. She grabbed my face, and I pressed her up against the wall. She stuck there in the corner, surrounded by the white tiles, and then slid down.

She stared like somebody who has suddenly died. The morning light came in through the window onto the splashed walls and mirror.

I turned off the water and there was silence. We looked at each other.

Then she looked aside, at nothing in particular.

"You've got ten minutes. I'm leaving in ten minutes," I said.

She got out of the bath and started to take off her soaked shirt and underwear. Afterward she dried herself, put on panties, a T-shirt, pants, and a hoodie.

We got into the elevator.

We got into the car.

In Sopot she said, "Right, left, here." I dropped her near a building beside a lawn, and the sun glided on the morning frost.

She didn't say a thing when she got out of the car. She went along the path by the frozen grass, entered the shadows, and then the building.

It looked strange from the firm's white Golf. I stayed sitting in the car with the motor on. I looked up and saw birds on a power line. I remember I thought then that it would be nice to light a cigarette there, in the parked car, inhale deeply, and reflect on everything. I thought of the diesel rumbling in front of the building and whether to cut it, or to go. I lit a cigarette.

The smoke floated lazily in the light.

The lawn was frosty under the sun and shone in my eyes. I adjusted the rearview mirror and looked at myself. I searched my pockets for the bottle, tilted back my head, and put in some more drops. The diesel rumbled, everything shook. I kept missing, the drops fell into my eyes and all around. Then I shifted into reverse, turned around, and left. As I drove along Dubrovnik Avenue I kept saying: "I'm a rock 'n' roll rebel, I'm a rock 'n' roll rebel..."

Sometimes I see that bartender; he's been working in a bar downtown for a long time. When I go in, he nods as if he knows me, but he can't place me.

I don't really know why I go there. The place is all pastels and marble, the tables dark. I sit down and feel confined, like in the firm's Golf.

The car got stolen, it simply wasn't out in front of the building one morning. The honchos didn't believe me. "Who'd steal a jalopy like that?" they said.

If I'd known more I would have said so.

Now I work here nearby, and sometimes I go to that bar. I have a coffee or a beer, read a newspaper that doesn't interest me, or look around. There are watercolors on the walls: a town in the mist, horses, and abstract drip paintings. Someone put in a lot of time and energy, but it all has no identity.

ROBERT PERIŠIĆ

Something Flashed

HOT DAYS, HOT nights. Summertime, Dalmatia.

The small town was magically deserted, as if someone had left it there just for us. We were eating lasagna by candlelight, in a romantic spot. She was beautiful. Dark eyes, dark hair, white T-shirt. She was looking at me, in love.

I was having beer after beer. I had no appetite. It was the third night in a row that I'd taken the bus to come in to town. Paying for the ticket. There were fewer passengers each night.

She said, "Know what? One can survive anything. If one has to."

"Yes," I said.

"Relax, what are you afraid of?"

"Nothing."

"I used to imagine what it might look like. I always thought I wouldn't be afraid."

"Me too."

"Now I know. There is nothing I cannot survive. If they come. I will be able to remain polite, I will be able to talk to then, I will be able to be marvelous, you know. Go out with them, if necessary, I could do that too. I could sleep with them. Cook for them," she said. "But I'd be putting poison in their food! Little by little, slowly but surely. I could do it all with them because I hate them so. That's why I am not afraid of them. They can't do anything to me."

It sounded like she was talking about men.

"I know it sounds bad, but I hate them," she said. "I hate Serbs."

"Ah," I said, relieved. "Me too."

"No, you don't."

I have no idea how she worked it out. Generally, I thought my chances were better if I hated Serbs. But you can't always pretend.

"Imagine an invasion," she said.

She was imagining it pretty romantically, I could see it in her eyes. Blame that on heroic history and the movies.

"Yes," I said. "We don't have much time. Shall we go to your place?"

She dangled her keys over the table.

We walked along the seafront, alone, under a gentle moon. I was holding her lightly by the waist. I whispered in her ear about how beautiful she was, as if it were a secret. The sea and her hair were fragrant.

I could do it all with them because I hate them so. It's strange when a woman you're about to go to bed with tells you that. Strange times. Every night was different.

We walked into her apartment and she lit a candle by the bedside. As I said: romantic. There was a radio there too. I also have one by my bed at home. I turn it on so it drowns out the sounds of sex.

A religious painting hung above the bed. And on the wall opposite, a picture of her grandparents.

"Grandma is dead. I should move out of my parents'," she said.

"Great," I said.

"Don't say that."

"Sorry."

I gave her a serious look and kissed her. We were on the bed. She had enchanting breasts. I started looking for a radio station with music. There was just news.

"Wait," she said. "Leave it!"

"Come on, we're not going to listen to. . ."

"Leave it on. They're talking about us."

"Us?"

"Quiet!" she shouted.

"Are you nuts?"

"They said something about a warship and they were mentioning us."

"Us?"

"Yes, but I can't hear because you keep talking over it!"

Suddenly an air raid siren howled.

"Shit," I said.

It was my first air raid siren ever. And hers. She blew against the candle's flame and it went out.

"What now?"

"Come on, lie down," I said.

"On the floor?"

"Anywhere. There's no time to lose."

But she got up and looked out of the window through a gap in the curtains.

I said, "No one can see you, we're in utter darkness."

"You think they don't see in the dark?" she said.

She thought I was naïve.

"Who?"

"You idiot, the ship is there," she hissed.

Something flashed at sea.

"Don't be angry," I said.

"Don't be so loud!"

I went to the window. I couldn't see a thing. I wanted to open the balcony door.

"Jesus, no! No!" she wailed, dragging me back to the bed.

Something flashed at sea.

"You see," she whispered.

"We're done for. Let's make love, now or never!"

But something else happened: she started to cry. I embraced her and whispered that everything would be all right.

I was having a tough time. My dick was getting hard and soft in that hot dark night, under an air raid alert.

"Okay, it's okay, everything will be okay . . ."

If I had managed to go out onto the balcony and seen what was up, it would have been easier, but like this I was starting to freak out from the world outside, and I curled up against her. I wondered if I loved her. I was wondering how it was going to end, where this was going. My dick was getting hard and soft in the dark. This was not improving matters.

She was crying. There was no way of stopping her. When it flashed again, she yelped and ran into the bathroom. I went after her and knocked something down on the way. She was sitting in the dark. I closed the door and turned on the light because there was no window in the bathroom.

Her makeup was all over her face.

"We're safe here," I said and hugged her tight.

I wish I was miles away from here, I thought. Still, I was right there, shut inside a bathroom. And now I really didn't know what was going on outside. Maybe they're really attacking, I thought. I imagined them silently surrounding the building. I also had seen too many movies. She was trembling. I wanted to say something calming, something manly, but she looked strange, her face was twisted, her eyebrows, eyes. . . Hysteria.

ROBERT PERIŠIĆ

It frightened me. The war had started. In that windowless bath-room. I hugged her again and repeated constantly: "All right, all right, calm down."

She was talking about her mother through her tears. Her mother, who had sacrificed everything for her without a word, never complaining, her good old mother, and where was she, what was she doing? She was crying and talking, and she seemed to be looking for the door with her eyes. She had come here to have sex with me, rather than being home at a time like this. Her mother would be beside herself with worry! She would be the death of her own mother! She had already killed her. Oh, mother! She was finished.

"We have to go to their house now, now, we have to go!" she wailed through her tears. "Jesus God, forgive me please!"

I didn't know what to do.

"Jesus, where will I go?" I said.

Jesus said nothing.

She was trying to unlock the door. She kept missing the keyhole, making a racket in that ghostly silence. This was not helping my nerves.

"Jesus, forgive me," she pleaded.

I grabbed her firmly and turned her toward me. I put my palms on her cheeks and hissed, "Shut up! Calm down!"

She was breathing like she would hyperventilate.

"Calm down!" I said.

She calmed down. Sobbed every now and then, resting her head on my chest. We stood like that for a moment or two, as if on a stage. I forgot, or I possibly didn't know, that I should speak. He who speaks more wins. One needed to charge forth.

But I forgot to speak.

She suddenly pushed me away. As if I were the enemy.

"Open the door or I will scream," she screamed.

I opened the door. She ran out.

I stood at the door of someone else's apartment in utter darkness, my dick limp.

I closed the door.

I went into the bedroom, looked outside. The beach, pine trees, the darkness of the sea. I sat on the bed. Everything was shut, the room smelled of old furniture. That thing I'd knocked down was the radio. Patriotic songs were fuzzily coming through from somewhere on the floor. Over there in the dark hung the picture of her grandfather and grandmother, the grandma being the last to die, probably here, on this bed where I was sitting. I was sweating.

I went to the kitchen. I opened the fridge and the inside light came on. There was no beer or alcohol of any sort, just light. I was gripped by terror.

I ran out of the apartment and down the stairs.

You could see things outside. The trees swayed in the wind.

Something flashed again.

I ran. The silence was absolute. Only my running was audible, and my breathing. After a few blocks, I spotted her. She was walking like someone who was terribly afraid.

She turned and saw me.

I walked quickly toward her.

I was following her, breathless, like some pervert.

"Forgive me," I said, not really knowing why.

She was quiet and looked ahead. We walked side by side.

"Hey," I said.

"What do you want?"

"I didn't want anything to happen to you."

"Don't worry," she said.

"What have I done?"

"Nothing. It's my fault... for getting involved with a kid." She stopped and looked at me with pity. "It's not your fault."

I was silent and looked down. I might not have played this game normally, but I had nowhere to sleep that night. And those ships were flashing. And anyway, where was my mother at that moment?

I hobbled after her, humble.

We reached her parents' house.

She said she'd sneak me into her bedroom.

"Are you sure?" I said.

"Don't worry," she said.

I kissed her dramatically.

She took me inside, we sneaked up the stairs, she led me into her room, and left me there. She was going to let them know she was home.

I stood in the dark, waiting, thinking, What if someone else comes in? I didn't give a shit about the ships, planes, Serbs, but I was tiptoeing and breathing without making any noise. I hid in a corner behind the wardrobe, in the dark. I thought, if her mother came in she would scream, and the dad would run up thinking I was the enemy, or at least that I was a drug addict and a tramp with nowhere to go at a troubled time, and had no respect for a home, his or my own, or generally for parents or God; in any case it would be clear I was a stranger, a suspicious element by all accounts—a thief, a criminal in the dark behind the wardrobe, a murderer, an enemy, an invader, an aggressive individual who wanted to bed his daughter. He'd be thinking all of this. There would be some truth in it. And he'd squash me in that corner like a spider.

Ten minutes passed. In the dark behind the wardrobe, I really felt like a secret agent.

Now I was not only afraid of her dad. After all, I thought that special police forces could come into the house and conduct a search. This seemed logical. If only they knew I was there. Because I am the worst. The head of the household would be tortured until he gave me away. Possibly the rest of the family too. But they wouldn't get anything from them. Except if they caught her and tortured her. It was dangerous for everybody.

Someone opened the door.

I stepped out with my hands in the air. I couldn't see a thing.

She hugged me, started to kiss me, and threw me on the bed. She said, "The ship, it's ours! Ours! Our soldiers took it!"

She was singing with delight.

"Thank God," I said. We unzipped in a hurry.

It's better that he came in sooner rather than a little later. But he came in then. Her dad with a flashlight. He pointed it at us. At me.

Everyone was shocked. Silence.

"Listen. . ." I said, embarrassed, ready to confess all.

"This is my friend," she said, and said my name.

Silence again.

Her father was a mountain of a man. But he was not aggressive. He was shy. I could see that he wished he hadn't come in. He was especially embarrassed for me. Or at least that's how it seemed. He turned off the flashlight.

I thought about saying, "Everything is okay," but kept quiet.

He walked to the window and looked out. He said, sadly, "I wanted to show you something."

We zipped up in a hurry.

"Look outside," he said in a fatherly manner.

He was also talking to me, which made me feel better.

We stood next to him by the window. I strained my eyes. I really wanted to see something, honor this trust he was showing me. To say something like "yes" or "I see." And then we could all talk about it, connect that way. Because war is for everyone.

And actually, there was something moving on the road.

"Our side has liberated an army barracks in Ploce," he said. "Those are trucks full of weapons."

We were as quiet as children.

"I was going out, to have a look. I wanted to show you," he said to his daughter, sadly.

I thought he'd be happier if I left and so liberated his daughter than if the army liberated another ten barracks. It seemed like his greatest desire, and I wanted to please him.

"Can I come along," I asked, "to have a look?"

"Let's," he said, tired.

She wanted to come along too.

"No," he said. "You see what's happening out there."

I said, "Bye, see you."

He and I went down the stairwell. The flashlight lit the way. We said nothing. We walked through the courtyard in complete darkness. The gate squealed. We reached the road. The trucks crawled very, very slowly.

"Look at them," he said.

"Yes," I said. "It's madness."

"Madness," he repeated, as if the word had struck him as important.

I went in the other direction. I did not sneak off, but walked with my back straight. Then I bumped into a bench, and sat on it. I was sitting erect, like a blind man.

Minutes passed. I thought about lighting a cigarette, but then thought better of it.

Weapons are passing along. Now you have to have a reason. For everything. For sitting on a bench, for lighting a cigarette. Everything is a sign. I sat there, inconspicuous.

A dog started barking at me. I walked inside the house. Sandra and her sister were sitting there. Two other guys came in and sat down. Sandra was saying something. Then her face vanished. It went out, there was nothing on it. It was uncomfortable, horrible, instead of her face, a jumble of cubes was lit up.

I don't know who said it, but someone did: "What's going on with your face, for God's sake?"

She was startled, as if she knew, as if it wasn't the first time this had happened. She ran to the bathroom.

Hopefully things will be better, I thought.

"Her face is all over the place," her sister said. She was crying. "She'll never get married."

Sandra came back from the bathroom. Her face was still a mess. But now you could see how. Everything was loose. She smiled at me, hopeless and horrified, as if saying, It's over, this is how it will be from now on.

The barking woke me up. I was cold. I pushed the dog away. I felt crumpled. People passing by glanced at me, but rushed past. They didn't want to meddle.

Translated by VESNA MARIC

ROBERT PERIŠIĆ

Debt Collectors

BRACO HAD LONG forgotten how he and Joško debated about which car they'd own when they grew up. Sanja had also forgotten, even though she witnessed the conversation.

"I'll have a varburg!" said Braco. His father had a Wartburg.

Despite the fact that Joško's father had an ancient sky-blue Volkswagen, nicknamed Beatly, he said, "When I grow up I'll drive a BMW!"

Braco thought this impossible and said, "Who'll pay for that?"

Joško said, "If my dad has a Beatly, I'll have a BMW!"

Braco found this very odd. He was convinced that Joško was only saying this for Sanja's sake, so that she would fall in love with him, and so that they could get married when they grew up. Sanja was Braco's cousin, but he was still jealous.

"How do you mean?" Sanja asked Joško.

Joško said, "My granddad didn't own a car at all, and my dad has one. We always have more. So I'll definitely have a BMW, and even an airplane. Because I'll have more than my dad. The new kids always have bigger things."

This got Braco thinking, and for the first time he felt pleased to be little, because they were these "new kids."

"Then I'll have a Mercedes!" said Braco. His world had changed. In a moment.

"I'll have a big baby doll with a stroller, and a skyscraper!" Sanja declared.

Then Joško said, "Let's get naked."

Braco agreed.

Sanja ran away, she didn't want to. A pity. Perhaps because she was a year older. But she must have spied on them. And it was probably her that called Braco's mom, who found them naked, the new kids, and spanked Braco so badly he forgot the entire episode.

Joško was spanked by his mom, and Sanja by hers, because she had been looking at the boys. And everyone forgot everything. Or so it was thought.

So, Braco doesn't remember this, and he also has no idea about the way kids today think. It's a difficult thing to know, how can anyone know it? He doesn't know what his little boy is looking at, what he sees. Sometimes he thinks the kid gets it, but says nothing, although he was supposed to start talking by now. He says a word here and there, as if he gets it. Sometimes he does get it, you can tell. But it's as if he's not there.

"So why doesn't he talk yet?" he asked his wife.

"Why are you asking me?"

"How old is he now?"

"Almost three."

"Shit."

The boy glanced at him as if he understood.

These are different times, who knows what he might know? Maybe the boy understands that Joško didn't buy an airplane, or a BMW. Maybe he knows that Joško had been driving his old man's Yugo, which he'd bought when the Beatly fell apart, until he was recruited into the army mid-war, and until he overdosed the first night he was let out on a visit home. This counted as if he'd died in the war, and so his unit paid for a prominent in memoriam dedicated to him to be printed in the local newspaper every year.

Braco had not been friends with Joško for a long time by then, perhaps because he had carried on thinking about cars. And Joško had turned into a rocker and had friends in town.

And, believe it or not, Braco had never forgiven Sanja, even though he'd forgotten it all, for not seeing her naked and for the fact that she'd told on them. They behaved as if they hadn't grown up together, never mentioned a thing from their shared past. She married Stipe Leko, who is approaching right now, while Braco is lying under a car.

"What's wrong with it?"

"I don't know, it suddenly starts shuddering, as if it's running out of petrol," said Braco.

"You should get rid of it," Leko said.

"It's okay. Just need to get the electrics sorted."

Leko lit his cigarette suspiciously.

"Yeah, it's just the electrics. Nothing else. But there are no real fucking mechanics left."

"No one wants to take the fucking time," said Leko, blowing out smoke.

He smoked strong cigarettes and wore dark sunglasses. Sometimes he beat Sanja. She once stammered something about it, but Braco had just watched her numbly.

"No real mechanics left," said Braco. He liked those kinds of statements, passed on by the elders.

"No one wants to fucking bother," said Leko.

"I went over to Burić. I watched how he works, he's screwing it on by hand, can you believe it? I didn't want to say anything. I got in the car and wanted to see whether it would work. By the time I got home it had started spluttering. You get it, he's fixing the electrics with one hand and in the other he's holding his cigarette."

"No one has the energy to bother anymore," said Leko. He had an almost new black BMW.

"I told him later: this isn't how it's done, man! No one will come back, I told him. I won't come back!" Braco said.

"What'd he say?" Leko asked with scorn.

"Give me a smoke," Braco said after wiping his hands on his trousers. He lit up. "Him? Nothing, as if I'd said nothing. You know what mechanics are like, you can't talk to them."

"Yup," Leko responded.

"They're always looking elsewhere, then turn around and leave as if you're not there at all. For fuck's sake, I said to this Burić. For fuck's sake!"

Leko squinted. "And?"

"He opened the till. Gave me a fiver and went to wash his hands."

"No one wants to fucking bother, I tell you."

"Yeah, I heard you the first time," said Braco, closing the hood. "Let's go."

"Hang on, let me wash my hands," Braco said.

Later, on their way to Opuzen, after a long silence, Leko laughed and said, "Hey, don't get mad, but I heard, I mean, I don't know if it's true, that the only thing your kid can say is Tudjman."

"What?"

"He can't say mommy, or daddy, just Tudjman."

"Who told you that?"

"Oh, I just heard."

"People talk shit."

"Don't get angry. It doesn't matter."

They rode in the black BMW and listened to Severina. Braco looked around. His thoughts spun and shook this way and that, just like the Croatian highway. At some point he found himself wondering whom Severina was fucking. Severina was hot. Then he thought of his wife. His wife, realistically speaking, was young, good looking, but somehow she had evaporated. That's what it seemed like to him, as if she didn't exist anymore. As if she had ceased to exist. He tried to recall what it had been like before she'd evaporated. He remembered, yes, that she talked loudly and laughed, that her body felt real under his and that she had inspired a kind of will in him, a will to move, to really go somewhere without thinking. That might even be what he did. She still talks in a loud voice, and he tries not to get irritated. And every time he remembers that, that will, the only thing he thinks of is that word: evaporated. They had reached a certain point, and he now felt alone and angry, like after Hajduk lost an important match, long ago. Even that's gone. Important matches. Just boredom and irritability.

Plus, he had no idea whom Severina was fucking.

"What do you think, would Severina evaporate if you were married to her?"

"What?" Leko was startled.

"Like, you see through her, you don't see her."

"Yeah, of course she would."

Braco fixed on a random spot ahead, as if checking how far it was to Opuzen.

"I don't know."

"Don't talk shit," said Leko.

They didn't talk for the rest of the drive. Leko changed the music. Put on an old crooner.

Leko was one of those people who sat straight up when he drove. He had a golden chain around his neck, with a cross upon which a small golden Jesus was dying, and on his forearm, the part where the skin was white and soft, he had a tattoo of a dark circle leaning onto an Eiffel Tower. Looking at it Braco couldn't gather what it meant, and then it occurred to him that it represented a layer over an older tattoo that contained an A. Maybe an ex, or an ex-army.

Leko looked at Braco, but Braco had already averted his gaze.

They found the man. Leko had told Braco what was going on, who the guy was. The guy was an owner of something. He had small eyes and a big belly and was in his fifties. They stood in the corridor of his apartment, and the guy stood in front of them and blinked. He was a big guy, but he was crapping himself, looking at Leko's gun.

It had to begin. In that narrow, wood-paneled corridor with fuzzy lighting, Braco was thinking about how it had to begin, you had to reach out, hold on to something, while an indecisive clock ticks inside your head, like in those moments when you're sitting in a wood-paneled booth with fuzzy lighting, and opposite you is a girl that you're still unsure if she's up for it or not, so you have to finally reach out for fuck's sake, grab her by the wrist, the first time, you have to do it.

That ticking clock of indecision in your head, that's the present moment.

In the corridor. Braco took the fatso's arm and twisted it forcefully. The guy squealed.

Then Leko put his gun in his belt and slapped the fatso.

And again.

And so on, and so on, and they agreed they'd come back in five days.

Five days later, Leko again found Braco messing with the car. He didn't say hello.

Braco spread grease removing paste on his hands and said, "My wife's not home."

"So?"

"There's no one to look after the kid."

"Where the fuck is she?"

"Work."

"Why didn't you let me know? I'd have looked for someone else."

"I forgot. I only just realized she's not here."

"Bring the kid."

Braco kept cleaning off his hands with the paste.

"There's loads of space in the back seat," Leko said.

"What?"

"He's coming with us," said Leko.

The kid was saying something like, "Wooooooooo. Toooooo. Woooooo." In fact, written like that it looks weaker than it is, but which sounds can convey that hissing? Hissing. That's better. Hissing. Whooooo. Leko was annoyed. He was silent. Braco was enraged. He didn't know at what. At his wife? At Leko?

The kid was saying something like, "Vootoo, vootoo, vootoo."

What car will this new kid drive?

Leko drove, and the kid looked around, hissing and spitting on everything.

They left the boy to play in the car.

The fatso was expecting them. He still had small eyes and a big belly. This time he also had money. They stood in the corridor of his apartment, and he invited them to sit. He was a big guy, a real boss. He was in a very good mood. He gave them the money and even asked them to work for him.

Braco said, "What?"

Leko said, "We'll be in touch."

They stopped for a drink on their way back. They also snorted some of Leko's coke. Their mood improved, all in all. Leko gave Braco his share of the money. They sat in an empty bar by the road and drank.

Braco said, "What about the kid's share?"

"What?"

"His money."

Leko bared his teeth. That was a smile.

"The kid was with us too."

Leko found this very funny. So did Braco.

"He was with us, was he not?"

The boy was looking up from his chair, his eyes wide, like a clever little dog. Braco thought he was getting it.

"Okay," Leko said, looking up at the ceiling, his mouth agape, as if considering whether to laugh. "If he says . . ."

"What? What's he supposed to say?"

"Tudjman. If he says Tudjman, he gets a cut."

Braco didn't get angry. It seemed like a fair deal. Surprisingly, he found it quite amusing. He was in a terribly good mood. He was high.

"Go on, say, Tudjman," Braco said to his son.

The boy just looked at him.

"Tuuu-djman, Tuuudj-man, Tudj-tudj-maaan," Braco said in some ridiculous mimicry of child speak, so that the boy would get it.

Nothing.

The boy was opening his mouth, but was not interested in making a sound, just moving the muscles.

"Tuuuuuudj-maaaaan. . ."

Leko burst out laughing.

Braco looked at him and thought something like, The world has gone mad.

"Tuuuuuuuudj-maaaaan," Leko started echoing, bending over on the chair and laughing hysterically.

"That's it! Just like Uncle Leko says," Braco whispered to his son.

"Tuuuuuuudj . . ." Leko was saying, pouting his lips, then relaxing his jaw into "maaaaan."

He was staring at the boy. The boy appeared to be confused.

Then Leko raised his face sneering, wondering why this was amusing him so much, and how he and Braco understood each other so well in that laughter, like they had never understood each other before, it's really fucking strange, he thought.

The waitress watched them from the bar, and she was finding it funny, although she had no idea what the joke was.

Now both of them were howling before the child who had opened his eyes wide, eyes framed with long, curled eyelashes, and watched these two creatures smelling of car fumes, opening their mouths: "Tuuuuuuudj-maaaaaaan. Tuuuuuuudj-maaaaan."

"Tuuuuuuudj"—they made a slight pause, and carried on—"maaaaaan. . ."

And the child started smiling, *heh*, laughing, *heh*, *heh*, but did not speak. As if newly awoken, shaking his head and his entire body, in a sudden euphoria of eyes, little teeth, and the hearty laughter of children, with a convulsion of his gentle palms, he started waving his arms, but it was clear he would never fly.

Translated by VESNA MARIC

The Visit

ĐANI AND I went up to Zagreb. We were there for a few days, and we went to visit Tandara at Vinograd Hospital. He was being treated there, like, for a heroin addiction.

We searched for him, toured all the wards, but he was nowhere to be found. Nobody had heard of him. You won't believe it, but I found out later that he lied about going to get detoxed. He actually went to Zagreb to help a relative with a job there. Bricklaying, for a daily wage. But going to rehab earned him more credit. He told his tragic story to everybody. That's how he is. He was ashamed to go bricklaying, so he lied and said he was going to get off the dope. And everyone, like, felt sorry for him. And he acted some schizo crisis when we saw him off at the bus station. I mean, he was just going to do some bricklaying in Zagreb.

I remember we stayed a while there at the station. I mean, what a fucked-up life. We had no idea he was in so deep. And everyone asked what was wrong with him. We explained. He hung out with Alen that summer, and they kinda got hooked together. You can imagine. Probably he didn't even give himself a proper jab.

It doesn't matter.

And here's what happened at the hospital there: Đani and I inquired about him, like, and nobody knew a thing, but we were stubborn because he told us that's where he was going. Who could have imagined the jerk would tell us such a blatant lie, and so at one point we found ourselves in the drug addiction, alcoholism, and general psychiatry department.

It's nicely organized there, you know, a four-story building. We asked the nurses about him, and they all asked us for a smoke. No problem: I had a few packs in my rucksack for Tandara. So I handed out cigarettes, a queue formed, and Đani started baiting the gals, I mean hitting on them. He flirted with them all at once, as if he was in a club, you know what a seducer he is, he has no equal. I mean, ten to fifteen of them, no idea, I felt there were even more. Đani was in his element—shooting his mouth off, sure, but he was kinda witty.

So I was sharing out the smokes, as if it was my job, and I asked them about Tandara. The nurses at the front desk tore us to pieces, but I went on asking. 'Cos I reckoned he'd at least been there at some point. Maybe they'd moved him somewhere. I was worried, like, that something might've happened to him, that he might've done something stupid and been transferred to the loony bin in Vrapče or Jankomir. We heard that was where they sent people like that in Zagreb.

"He's almost seven-foot, sure you know him," meaning Tandara, but the nurses just looked at me.

I kept giving out the smokes. Some nurses asked for two or three, and then came again.

"Come on, shit, this is no good. When are we going?" I said and looked at Đani.

But by now he was pawing around with one of the nurses. Around the waist a bit, like, and on her butt. What do they see in him, I always ask myself. He'd get on my nerves if I was a woman. I mean, as is he gets on my nerves a bit. But, man, she was sure ready for the Richard. She had the itch. And, even better, the woman looked—wow!

She shook her hips, writhed. She was hot and wanted it.

"Let's go there a bit," she said to him, meaning round the back of the building.

Probably a dope skank. Đani winked at me, made a funny face, with his hand on her cute butt, and they were gone. Okay then, why should I care? Let him, I thought. It was no skin off my nose, I'd wait. Naturally, you always have to wait for him. I assumed the two of them would go, you know. But then all the nurses started heading off too. I didn't understand where they were going. Hell, I thought in the end, I'm going too.

That's why I got there a bit late.

I arrive, and what's going on? He's still nicely kneading her butt, and his other mitt slides into her penalty area. Her eyes are cheerful. Except that in her hand she's holding a switchblade. No idea where she got it from, but they're horsing around with it. They laugh. And Đani is still in his element. He fondles her breasts. I mean, you can see them. She's wearing a T-shirt and her nipples are sticking out. The other women are snickering. Some are young, others are older. Hm. . . I could start with one myself, there's one very pretty one, she smiles at me, and I look at her, but I think, What if she's loony? I mean, it's no problem if she's a drunk or junkie. . . What a beauty, you know, it's unreal.

I look at Đani again. His bird is constantly jerking around with that little knife. And she jabs it at his left breast, like just for a joke. But it rebounds.

He looks at her. She's smiling like before. As if to say: come on now if you're cool and you've got the balls, join in the game, it's such fun here, let's see you. Đani, like, laughs for the audience. He's a maniac too, he's as cool as a fucking cucumber. So he starts groping her again. But she jabs him once more with the knife, all a nice bit of fun. Now he stops a bit.

"Hey, gimme the knife," he says to her, still reasonable, like.

She's sexy, but there's a strange glint in her eyes.

"Girl, everythin's all right," I try to reassure her.

"Hey, gimme that!" Đani says to her, and she waves the blade in front of his face, a bit crazily, like come and get it.

He grabbed her arm. And with the other moved to pry open her hand. Man, did she holler! All of a sudden, everything turned around. I've no idea whether he let her go or she tore away, but now she stood in front of him with the knife and glared. She moved toward him, and I saw panic in his eyes.

"Come here, playboy," she snarled.

I didn't feel entirely sorry for him because he'd always been an insatiable womanizer. But I had to try and help, right?

His eyes flitted around, he caught sight of me, and backed away.

"There, see," I wanted to say to him. I approached. But now she turned on me with the knife. She wasn't joking around.

I was packing shit, I really was, and I dunno how, but I was fast. I grabbed her arm and twisted it, and the switchblade fell to the ground. I kicked the blasted thing away. But her other hand was free and she clawed me with her nails. I let her go and felt my face: blood. She bent down, going for the knife. Đani stepped on her hand. Her eyes sought help.

I whipped around and looked at the other nurses. They were all looking at me. That was a long, long moment: they were all around. And obviously they weren't on our side. I could only beg them not to join in. You know, silently, gesticulating.

Đani managed to kick the knife away.

It lay in front of me. I had it.

I edged away. My legs were wobbly and I could hardly run.

ROBERT PERIŠIĆ

Finally the orderlies came charging in. They jumped on Đani's nurse and held her down. She howled and screamed.

Later I rang around and dug up the number of Tandara's relative in Zagreb, and he told me that Tandara was bricklaying. As if it was one of the most normal things in the world.

You don't know if you feel more like laughing or crying. What sort of weirdos do I mix with, I thought.

"Tell him we were lookin' for him, and we got into a big mess," I told the guy.

"Hotshots like you? Fuck!" he said. "If you wanna come an' lay some bricks too—no trouble at all."

I told that to Đani, for the hell of it.

He said, "You know what? I've been thinkin', we oughta get serious."

And he went off to lay bricks. Jeezus.

Dementia

EVER SINCE THEY told Jakov it was best he not hoe the vine-yard anymore, he hobbled around slowly in his old suit, with his walking stick, and said hello to his acquaintances. Usually he didn't have much to say, a few words of greeting and that was all. Still, he would sit for a while in Baldo's store or out in front of it, depending on the weather. Later he went to have a look at the vineyard. One day, as he was standing in the vineyard, a Renault 4 drove up.

Jakov was surprised, then his face lit up. "Where ya been?"

"Hi, Dad," Miro said, wearing a spring shirt with a tie.

"What's up?"

"Get in, we'll go for a drive."

"Where to?" Jakov asked briskly, already fumbling around with the doorhandle.

Miro opened the passenger door from inside and said, "We're goin' to a nice place to pick up a nice form."

"A form?" Jakov squinted and glanced at his son. "Trust you to come at around lunchtime."

"We're gettin' the form, and then I'm takin' you to lunch," Miro said.

"In these old rags?"

In town, Miro told Jakov to wait. Jakov sat in the Renault 4 and looked through the window. His son came back and hopped in. He wasn't the youngest for such antics anymore either, Jakov thought.

"Goody," Miro chirped and started the car. "Now for a nice bowl of tripe."

Jakov pouted silently.

"Come on, Dad, you won't've served the Italian invaders in vain," Miro said cheerfully and shifted from third to fourth gear.

"I didn't serve them," Jakov bristled.

Miro had expected that. "Yes, you did, you devil," he said through a laugh. "You served them."

"I blinkin' did not!"

"Yes, you did, you told me so."

"I made it up!"

"Mother told me too."

"She don't know a damn thing," Jakov snorted and fell silent.

"There's money in it, Dad, don't you get it?"

They sat in Pod Odrnom, slurping their soup and slowly chewing the tripe with their false teeth. Miro poured him wine diluted with water.

"You know, Miro," Jakov said seriously, "I've got this here pension, the veteran pension, 'cos I fought with the Partisans, where I fucked up my leg, and we won the war. You know that!"

"Yes, but now the Italians have decided to grant a small pension to everyone who was conscripted into their army. Backdated all these years, do you understand?" Miro said, looking at his father.

"I didn't fight for them, I didn't win the war with them. I ran away—I deserted!" Jakov exclaimed.

"So what? So what if you deserted?"

"So what?" Jakov swung his arms. "Then, then… forget it!"

"Want me to tell you how much it is all together?"

Jakov looked blankly. There were still two or three he would be ashamed to tell.

"Oh, we've all gotta die sometime," Jakov said, looking at his son.

"Dad, stop the bullshit. It'll all go into your account. No one will be stealin' it from you."

Miro knew his old man had no way out. It was moolah, and money didn't stink. He was hemmed in by his badgering daughter and the imploring blackmail of his grandchildren.

"I'd be ashamed. I'm not gonna go beggin'!" Jakov shook his head and huddled on the chair.

"It's not beggin', you're entitled to it. I'll go, I'll do the talkin'. You just need to say, *Sì*!"

Jakov flipped the plastic-coated menu over and over on the tablecloth.

"Okay then, *sì*, and the devil take it," Jakov grumbled and took an angry gulp of his drink.

When the waitress had wiped down the table, Miro took the form out of his bag, laid a large exercise book underneath it, and assumed the pose of a clerk.

"Were you conscripted?"

"Yes."

"Where?"

"Um, from home."

"Tell me first: Where were you stationed?"

"In Zadar. We'd been there less than ten days when I deserted."

"And before?"

"What do you mean before?"

"Before Zadar."

"I don't remember."

"You were only in their army for ten days?"

"Er. . . we were there longer, I dunno, that's what I've always said. Maybe it was a month or two. We were at some barracks, but outside under the sky, I remember, and one evening. . ."

"How long?"

"I dunno, all together I s'pose two or three months, somethin' like that, but they transferred me."

"How do you mean transferred?"

"Here and there," Jakov said.

"Just you, or everyone?"

"Everyone."

"What unit was it?"

"Infantry."

"I mean its name, number. We need that for the form."

Jakov became absorbed in thought, then he said testily, "I dunno!"

Miro looked at him. "Name of officer? We need that too."

"Oh, yes," Jakov gushed, "He was handsome. Middle-aged, but he acted more like a young'un, spruced up a bit, with a feather in his hat. An' did he like to yell, the fascist! An' we. . ."

"Do you remember his name?"

"Once he smacked me in the gob," he said, glancing at his son.

Who was still waiting for the name.

Jakov continued, waving his arms, "His name? Hm, it could've been Ernesto, Cristo. . .He could speak our language a bit."

Miro sighed. "Who of the people you know was with you then?"

"No one from here."

"Do you remember anyone at all?"

"I remember one small guy from Fiume, who deserted with me. Him an' me. . ."

"What was his name?"

"Ive."

"Did you see him afterward?"

"He got killed, didn't make it."

"When?"

"The next day. On the road. He went to ask for some food. I ran an' hid in the bushes. I saw him run, and then he fell. Oh Ive, Ive!"

"What was his surname?"

"I dunno. I dunno if I even knew it back then."

Miro leaned his elbows on the table.

"Dad, come on and think. Try to remember. Stop messin' around."

"Who's messin' who around? I told you everythin'!"

"You have to remember names, think!"

They sat like that for a while longer. Then Miro put the form back in his bag. He drove Jakov home. The next day his daughter Marija came. All the grandchildren came for the weekend. Jakov was quieter than usual.

"Grandpa, can you remember?" little Lucija asked him with a smile.

Jakov said nothing.

"Grandpa can't re-meeem-ber! Grandpa can't re-meeem-ber! Grandpa is *stupido*!" Lucija sang as she hopped around playing jump rope.

Several months passed. Many seniors had collected their Italian back payments, people said. Most of them kept the money in the bank, untouched, and went on living as they did before. It must be big moolah then, Jakov thought.

One evening, Jakov fell asleep in front of the TV—although it was a program about great discoveries—and dreamed of the seafaring Christopher Columbus, of himself, and of the famous

Partisan Ivo Ribar ("Yes, yes!" Jakov thought in his dream, "Yes, I'll remember!"), as well as some others; he could reel off the names and surnames of them all. They marched in Italian uniforms with Capitano Colombo at the fore, leaving the barracks outside Zadar, the sun was sweltering and oppressive, it filled his eyes, and Jakov sweated, the perspiration ran in streams, and he wilted under the weight on his back as if he would melt; then a horse whinnied in front of Jakov and there was a scuffle. He cast off his load and began to run away by himself, without Ive, and vanished into the luminous haze.

Jakov opened his eyes. He switched off the TV and went to bed.

Time passed, life went on like before, except that jokes were made at Jakov's expense here and there. About how he lost the money. Jakov paid it no mind. He hobbled around like before in the greasy old suit, with his stick, and said hello to his acquaintances. At the end of his walk he went to have a look at the vineyard. He wasn't satisfied. He turned up in Baldo's store that day, for the first time in a long while, and sat down.

"Do you also think I'm an idiot?" he asked Baldo.

"Oh, who cares, Jakov," he said. "Forget about it."

With his voice raised Jakov said, "I know the names, but I'm not gonna say!"

"Well, sit and be quiet then," Baldo said.

Jakov went to Baldo's store the next day too.

"Baldo, they're all dickheads!" he said.

Baldo was adding up some figures on paper beside the till and didn't react.

Several days later, Jakov was sitting quietly in the store. Manda came in, wearing all black for her late Mateo, and said to Baldo, "I'll have two pounds of coffee, a bottle of oil, and detergent."

"Have you heard anything?" Baldo asked.

"Leave him be," Manda waved dismissively and nodded.

Jakov stood up abruptly, stuck out his chest, and declared, "I won't be a traitor! They might all be, but Jakov isn't!"

He sat down again.

"Jakov, leave politics out of it," Baldo said.

"Nope," he shook his head, "Jakov won't sell his soul!"

A few days later, Miro parked his car and got out with a combative air. It seemed he had heard the news.

"Dad."

Jakov made like a child caught up to no good, then said with a decisive swing of his arm, "I know the names, but I'm not gonna say!"

That resulted in bitter quarrels, with few words. In the end he threw everyone out. He didn't want to see anyone anymore, neither his children nor the grandchildren. He no longer went to Baldo's store and hardly said hello to his acquaintances. He would just hobble off to the vineyard on occasion.

Marija and Miro still came now and then, cleaned the house, and took his laundry. Jakov mainly kept quiet and stared blankly, full of spite. When he felt they were trying to lure him into talking, he would head off for the vineyard. His legs were very wobbly, but it was hard to hold him back. He broke free and cursed them.

He could no longer remember what they quarreled about, but he knew he had won.

That Way You'll Remember Me

THEY TOLD ŠPIRO that Grandpa was coming, and they told him that Grandpa had arrived. But instead of coming to their place he went to the hospital.

It was complicated. "Complications." He heard that word spoken softly so he'd understand it less. They too probably thought he was stupid, now after the peach therapist told them he was dysco and lexic.

As if he didn't know when someone was making things complicated. You can tell for sure when someone disses and complicates, although it's horrible to say so. But that's just what they did. They spoke like that as if everything could be concealed in words. They spoke words that wore away his attention.

It was a bit like with happiness, like at a birthday party, when the commotion stops you from concentrating on being happy. Only the other way round, because now it was sad. But it was utterly complicated because the sadness was in fact not allowed to be shown. This was so as not to dishearten a person who was ill, for example—that's how they said it. He realized it was about Grandpa. They had to behave almost as if everything was normal. As if it was sad but not sad. And they said it would get better.

He saw they had to behave as if it would get better. It seemed no one was able to do that and everyone behaved like stupid peach therapists. But that was just his feeling because no one spoke about it. They all pretended it would get better, but they couldn't behave that way because they had zero talent for acting.

Words were tricky at the best of times, and now they were really strange. Everything was mushed up in them—"better" and "worse," and "sad" and "hope."

That's how it was when he went with them to see his Dalmatian gramps in the hospital, when they told him in advance what he should ask him, so that's what he asked. They had to behave in a particular way, almost as if no one was ill and their visit just a coincidence. Everything was hidden in words, they covered it a bit like a bedsheet. Everything was hidden in words that wound around the thing like bandages, and you had to mind your words and you weren't allowed to ask Grandpa if he was going to die. Špiro asked them that in the car on the way to the hospital, and Mama got upset, turned around toward him, and said she didn't want to hear anything like that from him again. So everything kind of mingled in the words that are spoken and those that are not; and you had to mind both sorts so they didn't slip out accidentally. In the end, he thought too much about words and his behavior, and he was so afraid of making a mistake, and that's what he concentrated on, not on Grandpa. He was frightened because they were afraid of something, but no one said what it was. But it seemed not to be the only thing. There was a kind of fear there that made everything that was said and done feel strange and phony. It rubbed off on him and he could hardly wait for them to leave the hospital again. But that wasn't right. It wasn't fair to Grandpa. He was fond of his grandfather, and they had spent time together that summer. He loved to joke around with Grandpa, but he'd forgotten what about.

ROBERT PERIŠIĆ

As they were leaving, Špiro asked Grandpa, "Can I come and visit you by myself?"

He thought he would be able to talk with his grandpa if he was with him by himself. But his question caused puzzlement. His parents looked at him and then suddenly started to laugh. His grandpa started first, and then his parents. The laughter came like a dam burst. It seemed to hurt Grandpa to laugh, so he soon stopped, and they immediately stopped too.

Mama said, "But how will you by yourself?"

Grandpa then said to them, "You two go out so Špiro and I can have a bit of a chat."

When they were gone, Grandpa said, "They just bother, don't they? Tell me, what do you want to talk about?"

Špiro thought and was a bit afraid again. He said, "But don't tell them I asked you."

"I won't, you got it."

Špiro looked at him and thought again what mama told him he mustn't speak about. He contemplated how to ask the question. Then he dared. "Will you take me to the zoo again?"

"If I'm strong enough."

"Will you be strong enough?"

"I dunno, Špiro. Tell me again, I've forgotten: what's your favorite animal?"

"I like the elephants. And the monkeys."

"You know, if I'm strong enough, we'll go. But look, if I'm not, you can go to the zoo by yourself when you're a bit bigger. And when you're there, please tell the elephants and the monkeys that I said hello. Pick an elephant you like and a monkey that laughs. Will you remember?"

"I will."

"And somethin' else. Now you've reminded me. Can I ask you another favor?"

"Yes."

"Whenever you see a donkey... You know a donkey?"

"I know."

"Every time you see a donkey, tell him I said hello. You don't have to do it aloud. If someone's listenin', you can say it inside. Will you do that?"

"Yes."

"Good, that way you'll remember me."

While he spoke, Grandpa rummaged with one hand in his nightstand, although the movements seemed to cause him pain.

"Wait, I'll find it for you," Špiro said.

"No, here, here it is. Take this money, it's for when you go to the zoo."

"You want me to save it?"

Grandpa looked at him and said, "No, don't save it—spend it. The main thing is I gave it to you."

"Okay."

"So, an elephant and a monkey. And a donkey, always. Will you remember?"

"I will."

"That's agreed then, my dear Špiro. Let's shake hands."

Grandpa held his hand for a long moment. Then he said, "Off you go, your mum and dad are waitin'. See you then."

The Lover

I MET ROZANA in town. She asked what I was doing now and if I had any news.

"Nope, nothing spectacular, but everything's okay," I said.

She said she was now a volunteer with a hotline. For people in crisis situations.

I didn't ask about her motives. Maybe I'm prejudiced, but I thought there could be some sorrow behind volunteering. Did that just occur to me or did I see it for an instant in her eyes? I don't know, and perhaps I don't need to know.

I knew Rozana hadn't been working for a few years, that she was busy with the kid, and that her husband earned a good income.

"It's good that you're active again," I said.

She was always intelligent, I cribbed her tests; there's no point sitting around at home when you've got a higher education.

"The hotline—what is it exactly?" I asked as we were having coffee.

We don't meet often, so we always stop for a coffee if there's time.

"It's a good thing," she laughed.

"What are the people like?"

"You mean the ones who call or. . ."

"Er, like. . . altogether," I said.

"There are usually two of us staffing the phones, and four on weekends. It's kind of psychological first aid for children and adolescents, but anyone can call."

"Hm." I made a face of wonder and admiration.

She now had her listen-to-this face and said, "This morning a woman called, and not for the first time. Get this: she calls from Šibenik, somewhere around there, with that accent, and she's married, has two children, and a lover. She calls the hotline for teenagers, I mean, we've told her that, but she says she's got used to us."

I'd kind of forgotten Rozana's stories. She always has one to tell.

"It probably makes her feel younger," I said.

"Yes, you could say that. I think she's around forty-five."

"What do you say to her?"

"Ha, I don't know. We're in the process of discussing that. I mean, she's mainly talked with one of my colleagues, but, you know, we can listen, you can switch over with your handset because it's standard that a supervisor listens in and we discuss things afterward. It's all like a training session for us. The supervisor only comes in once a week, and we don't speak often, but this other volunteer had already told us . . . Like, the woman has a lover and her life has turned upside down. She torments herself, she's married. . . She's at a loss. But the story goes that my colleague felt something wasn't right. The way the woman talks—you don't know what's really going on. She always has to break off at this or that point because someone comes in. My colleague wanted to tell her at the beginning not to call anymore, but she found it interesting the way the woman talks, like out of some stupid soap opera. And, get this, my colleague asks her at one point, 'This lover of yours. . . what kind of relationship are you in exactly?' 'What do

ROBERT PERIŠIĆ

you mean?' the woman asks. 'I mean, have you had sex with him?' 'No, no,' she almost took offense. 'I'm a married woman.'"

"That's a good one!" I said.

We both laughed.

Rozana continued. "She says she works in a place that's like a bar but isn't quite a bar, perhaps it's something in between a canteen and a bar, I don't know—it's hard to be sure because it's as if she doesn't want to describe it in detail. So she works behind a bar of some kind, and he probably works in the same building. And he comes in for coffee. She says they're on formal terms in the mornings, and chummy and cozy in the afternoons."

"How's that?" I nipped in.

"I don't know, perhaps it's different in the mornings. Business-like. He might be there with others. Maybe he's some big shot there, but that's all hazy. In any case, he drops by in the afternoons too. Then they're chummy and cozy, she says. Apparently he offers to buy her drinks in the mornings, which she isn't allowed to accept, but it's endearing. He talks with her about quite ordinary things, but nicely, she says. And he listens to what she says, it interests him."

"But do you believe her that they're not. . . I mean. . ."

"We thought at first that she was ashamed to say it. Or afraid someone else might be listening. Certainly she torments herself. But it's all in riddles. Like, she's gone way too far. We thought maybe she's not capable of saying it. Because we reckoned something must have been going on if she calls him a lover, right? You think you know what a lover is, but you don't. It seems there's no sex. But the whole thing's still going on. She's always called in the mornings so far, from work, always mysterious and all sort of antsy. The calls are anonymous, but she's so wary that she also beats around the bush, so you know she said something else before—some different little detail, as if to throw us off."

"She hasn't got it easy," I said.

"It's interesting that she's not unhappy. She's scared, yes, but I don't think she's unhappy, and she has that amorous tone from time to time. Essentially she calls because, like, she doesn't know what to think of herself. And where it's going. That's what interests her. You might think we can say that to her, but we're not that kind of hotline, if one exists at all. We take her calls nevertheless because we don't really know what's going on. Oh, and now she's on her annual vacation. So she's been calling from home to say how much she misses him. Plus today is Valentine's Day. So all four of us were on duty."

"Yes." I smiled a little startled. "Today really is Valentine's Day."

"She says she never talks so nicely with her husband, and they don't go out anymore because, like, she works in a bar and he thinks that's enough for her. Her lover gives her zest for life. I can't be completely sure, but I think that's the gist of it."

"Hang on, if she calls him her lover. . . Have they at least, I don't know. . . at least kissed?"

"I don't think so. The story is ridiculous, but when you hear it you can't laugh. . . I don't know why, but today I intervened. My colleague let me, and the adultress of sorts is so absorbed in her story that she didn't notice the change in voice at the other end. We're probably just an abstraction for her anyhow. So I asked her if she's ever talked with him about all this. She says, as if admitting something big, she asked him if he got the best coffee when he came in the afternoons. She says he answered, 'There are lots of places I could go, you know, but I like it here the best.' Then she crooned, 'How nicely he said that.'"

"Her lover is also a bit passive," I said with a smile.

"She says he's similar in being a bit ungainly, and that's just right for her. As if they were made for each other. I said to her today when she called, 'You should have a deeper conversation with him. A bit deeper.' She said she'd like to, as if she thought of it just then. 'Well tell him a bit more clearly how you feel. So you see how he reacts. When you're alone.' 'Oh, he's a man, I can't do that,' she says. She's a married woman. And he's married too, of course. She says he once told her he'd get a divorce if it weren't for the children. That's when she called us for the first time. It seems as if that's when the affair officially began. The next day he brought chocolate to share with their coffee, as if he knew. In any event, she thinks he feels the same way she does. And that they don't need to say everything, but that they understand each other all the same. But now she's on vacation, and it's Valentine's Day. And he didn't come at all on the two days before her vacation. She's started to worry something might have happened to him. Or that maybe he's given up on her. In fact, she's afraid he could leave her. She's afraid he could leave her, and I'm not even sure he knows. I mean, maybe the guy didn't twig—I wouldn't be surprised, especially if they're similar," Rozana said, leaning over the table.

"Yes, perhaps," I said.

She fell silent and looked at me.

I felt she looked at me for a long time.

"I told her in the end, 'Touch him. Just put your hand on his,' I said. All the other volunteers looked at me a little strangely. But, I mean, we are there to help sort things out for the callers."

And then—I don't know what got into me, it was a moment—I put my hand on hers. It was as if it moved there by itself.

She froze, then pulled her hand away and muttered, "What the...?"

"Sorry," I said and blushed. Then I rushed to add, because I owed her an explanation, "It's...it's as if I was under suggestion."

What nonsense I was blabbing, I thought; did I want to say I was hypnotized? But in a way I was.

Rozana opened her cigarettes and nervously took one. It fell to the floor. She picked it up but decided not to smoke it.

"Quit the kidding," she said and took another. I lit it for her. She watched my hand and blinked.

I thought of what else to say to get out of the predicament.

"What's your prognosis?" I said, not knowing what else to do other than pretend I'd woken up from hypnosis.

She glanced at me as if she accepted the move, and then continued almost as if nothing had been, but as if she was focused on the story again, not on me.

"I shouldn't have done that. I went too far. I damn well crossed a line. Basically I was persuading her to take a course of action. I mean, the woman is married and has children. Who knows what hell could be let loose. That was totally irresponsible. I have to take it back. How stupid I am! What was wrong with the way things were?"

She said that, staring past me, as if she had forgotten where I was sitting.

I didn't know what to say: everything I could think of seemed strange and ambiguous. She needed a while to register the silence.

Then she put away her cigarettes.

"She'll call again, she's on vacation, don't worry," I blurted as Rozana got up, and hastily added, "Let me know how it goes."

She stopped and looked at me for a long moment as if she was going to slap me.

Then her face softened and she said, "It doesn't interest you really. What is it to you?"

She put on her coat, took her umbrella, and headed for the door.

I had the impression that she walked a bit strangely, too upright.

And I looked around to see if anyone had noticed.

What, Straightaway?

NENA SAID, "I've thought it over."

She said that in the old Opel Ascona in front of the building where her best girlfriend lived. Then she tiredly got out of the car.

That surprised him. He thought they would talk some more.

A fortnight had passed, and still he kept fumbling around with his phone and glancing at it as if he was waiting. Then he thought he should call.

He searched for arguments for that, then he had counter-arguments, as if he was debating with himself. Why didn't she call? Why should he call her? Voices pro and contra rose in his head. But he felt that one of them should definitely call.

He had already called a few times, but then he had nothing to say.

In fact, the first time he told her to come back to him. He couldn't go on, he said.

That didn't go well, so later he called, repeatedly, and promised himself he'd be up to it. He stuck to ordinary topics, simply to see how things were and what was new.

What? He felt he couldn't know that in advance.

They always ended the conversations without any element of the unpredictable.

He tapped his foot under the table.

That day was probably the best for checking car listings, he thought. His Ascona had stopped recently in the middle of the road. A couple passed by as he was staring beneath the hood and running his fingers over the leads. He raised his head as if he was going to ask them something. They instantly began to laugh.

Later the Ascona started again, but he lost trust in it.

He went into town on foot. The walking did him good. He dropped in at the bank, and now he had his savings in his pocket. He bought a copy of the classifieds and sat down in front of the Hotel Dubrovnik for a beer. He got out a pen, read attentively, and circled a few possibilities. Eventually he stopped at one announcing that a small, rather old Honda sports car was for sale.

He knew what that car looked like. It was not what he'd had in mind. Then he tried to imagine himself in it. Maybe he'd feel different then.

But the price was still very high given the car's age, and the ad said: nonnegotiable.

He called the number and an elderly lady answered. He could trust her then. He asked about the Honda.

Her voice was almost cheerful, as if he'd paid her a compliment by calling.

Something in that voice told him he'd be rejected, but it was nice that he tried.

"Yes, yes, I think I'll come and have a look," Maris said. "Just tell me, please, if the price is absolutely nonnegotiable?"

The lady confirmed the price with an apologetic air as if that was the end of it.

Maris looked at his phone as if reconsidering.

Then he finished his beer in a few swigs, paid, and took a tram to the other end of the city to have a look at the car.

He arrived at the address and rang the intercom. It seemed no one was there. He had to ring several times.

The woman came down in a tracksuit. She obviously felt awkward about not being dressed and made up. He thought her advantage was melting away. He had taken her by surprise.

They headed for the garage. She went into a wide, dark corridor, while he remained outside. Then she drove the Honda out into the sun.

It was love at first sight.

Maris was no expert on aesthetics. He couldn't say if he found a picture beautiful or not, but with the car he knew.

Still, the price was grossly inflated.

Maris told the lady in the tracksuit he was offering fifteen hundred less. On the way there he had decided that would be his upper limit. It was a great offer for a car of that vintage.

"No, really. That won't do," she said.

"But nobody will offer you more. It's got a few years on the chassis," Maris objected.

She explained that the car had been looked after like a baby. Her husband's Hyundai stood outside in the rain, but her little Honda had always been in the garage. You could see it.

He raised his offer by seven hundred.

She shook her head. He felt the old fear that he'd look like an idiot because he didn't know how to haggle.

He offered three hundred more, five hundred below her price.

She looked him in the eyes and shook her head. "The price is 5,200 marks."

He frowned and said several times that it made no sense, that really...

She moved to return the car to the garage.

He offered three hundred more, and decided this time was the last. Surely she had to come down a bit too. Otherwise it would really put a hole in his finances. Besides, it was a round figure. She was bound to have been aiming for 5,000 when she asked 5,200.

She shook her head, but she was torn. She said she had to call her husband, he'd kill her because they'd agreed they wouldn't be going down.

Maris also shook his head and said, "You know, I have to make a call too. I don't know either what my wife's going to say."

He moved away to the edge of the parking area. A fairly strong wind was blowing.

He spoke into his phone. "Nena, the lady will only go down two hundred . . . You know, I'm not sure it's still worth it . . . What do you say Nena, huh? Is it worth it?"

When he went back, looking concerned, the lady sighed and said, "You know, to tell the truth, you look like a fine young man to me. It might seem strange, but really—I wouldn't sell it to a snot-nosed kid or a slob who'd ruin it."

Maris listened to her with a serious face.

"If I have to sell it, I'd rather it go to you."

Afterward she invited him to her apartment for a coffee. They went up in the elevator. When they entered the apartment, he shook her husband's hand. He was a gray gentleman with a kind face. She told him she had retired, her daughter had gone to America, and the two of them were now alone.

They sat down at a small table in the living room.

Staring at the floor, she said she bought the Honda in Graz, back when she used to work in Ljubljana.

Her husband added that they didn't need two cars. He didn't believe she'd truly sell that car, he quipped. He couldn't refrain from showing his satisfaction.

She sighed.

"So shall we go to see the notary?" Maris asked.

The lady looked at him. "What, straightaway?"

She glanced at her husband.

"Yes," Maris said, "I've got the money in my pocket."

Later, as they were going down in the elevator, her husband raised his hand and stroked her hair. Maris looked away.

She drove to the notary's. The gentleman followed in his car.

After they had settled everything, they went to a parking area for trucks. Her husband stayed in his car while the lady explained to Maris the various switches and buttons. Then she collected her things from the car.

Maris did a test drive in that vacant gravel lot. The gas was pretty responsive, it accelerated immediately. He did a few rounds there before driving out onto the road. The lady stood in her tracksuit and watched.

The wind raised a cloud of dust. A semi-trailer stood in the background, and above it the sun was setting between the distant high-rises.

He lowered the sun visor, raised his hand, and glanced at the lady. She had glasses and short, sparse hair. She was of medium build and on the chubby side. The sports car was evidently her final illusion.

He drove away and watched her in the rearview mirror as she stood there waving.

Over the next few days, he kept noticing pensioners on the streets. As if there were more of them than others.

The others were partly somewhere else, at least mentally.

Nena, for example, talked for years about the island where they used to spend the summer because she loved it so much. She planned to live there one day. She even spoke about it the long-past evening when they'd first met, so he originally thought she was born there.

When did he say that to her? Maybe a few months ago.

"Do you still think we'll live there?" he asked.

He had already texted her to say he was sorry. Later he thought that was in fact the end of it. But she didn't answer.

It was evening. His brother was going to call him any minute now. He had asked him to come and take the Ascona, which had been parked in the rain in front of the next building for a long time.

"Down south you'll be able to sell it—people know each other there. Here no one believes it."

"What?" Jakša said.

"You know, that the car's okay."

"You think it is?"

"So-so, but it's good, it still runs. It's just that right now it won't manage a long haul, so we'll send it on the train. You'll fix it up a bit, you know how," Maris said.

"It's no trouble for me, but . . ."

"Then please come and get it. The money's yours. I know it won't be much, but I can't sell it. I don't know how to haggle. I haven't even washed it. I plan to every day. . . It looks a real mess."

"But. . . are you okay otherwise?"

"Come and get it, I'll pay for your trip."

"Okay, okay. It's an Ascona 1.6, right?"

"Yes, 1.6 J."

"We'll sort it out."

Later he tried to explain the situation to his brother, who listened patiently. But he wasn't good at explaining things. He said it himself: he didn't understand anything anymore.

He wanted his brother to say how he saw it. Should he keep calling her, or not?

He talked a lot. He squeezed more details into the story, and then reached the end.

"Did she tell you she'd thought it over?" his brother asked. "Is that what she said?"

He looked at him. "Er, yes."

"Then what is there to talk about?" his brother said and spread his arms.

They'd had a bit to drink.

"Maybe I wasn't listening properly," Maris said, lowering his head.

The next evening they headed for the freight terminal.

Maris drove the Honda and his brother followed in the Ascona. He didn't know his way about town.

Maris drove slowly and glanced in the rearview mirror from time to time. He was afraid it could break down, now at the end.

A man with a flashlight was waiting in front of the open freight cars.

His brother showed him the ticket through the window, the man said something and then went ahead. His brother followed at walking pace and inched the Ascona into the bowels of the freight car.

Maris stayed at the barrier and looked into the darkness there.

Winks of the flashlight; the smell of metal, fine rain.

He took a few steps and felt tracks beneath his feet.

His brother emerged from the dark, almost walked past him, and then said, "It's you."

Is Sena X Stupid?

YOU CAN'T HAVE a conversation these days without someone mentioning her. It seems everywhere I go I talk about Sena X. I've met her, and she isn't even so bitchy.

People ask if she's stupid.

I already have a kind of feeling for her and I say, "Well, sort of, she is and she isn't."

The songs they write for her—they're not so bad. The masses lap them up. And her attitude. The botox lips, the low-cut tops, the lifted ass—they're not so bad either. She is what she is, and she hasn't got it easy.

But, I mean, I have to laugh. Sena X . . . you can't say she's super smart.

Here people seem to perk up, as if gossip relaxes their brain.

Variety shows are made for that. It's not as if they really interest you, but then some hot shit catches your attention.

I kind of know all that via Sara, although she'd rather die than be mentioned in the same sentence as Sena X.

Most of the time she doesn't answer the phone. Almost as if I'm to blame. Or we're all to blame, I don't know. Like, we've all disgusted her. If Sara wasn't such an old friend of mine, I don't think I'd have the nerve for her anymore.

And all because of Karlo.

Karlo was her boyfriend, and they had been going steady for a hundred years. That's how I know him. He studied acting, he was quite a regular guy, sort of, he was okay. He'd taken the entrance exam five or six times and was no spring chicken when they admitted him. And then, before he'd even finished his degree, they invited him to host that show. I don't know quite what to call it: something between a quiz show and a proper program. Fancy gimmickry mostly. It doesn't matter. In any case, things then became too constricted for him.

Like, I'd go to their place for coffee, us two girls would sit at the table. I'd see him fidgeting on the couch, as if he were bouncing. Then he'd get up and pace about the apartment. He'd peer out the window.

He was always joking and making fun at her expense. And she at his.

I was neutral: I'd laugh at whatever was funniest.

Then it became a bit awkward for me. I saw she wasn't playing anymore. But he kept on. I'd smile and look away.

Sara just watched him. She'd probably had enough already.

She told me later that he'd said in a strange way that it was boring. He said it in a funny rhinal voice, as if it wasn't him speaking but was for fun. *How boring it is*, and that little voice, she imitated him. But he must have overdone it. Some jokes become serious. I thought about that later, how that little voice first hatched out of him like a little chick. Sometimes you don't have the courage to really think what's in front of you. First of all that little voice was speaking.

I think the thing was that the quiz show gained him admirers. Because some girls even asked me what he was like, and they said he was handsome. And I'm sure there were plenty of other girls. They don't have anything else to think about.

And Sara—you can't go treating her like that. Two months ago she called me. I was on the tram just then. She was kind of in shock.

"I kicked him out," she said.

"Where is he?" I asked stupidly, not knowing what else to say.

"I kicked him out... No idea where he's gone."

"Seriously?"

"What does he expect? He's become some starlet, so he craps on all the time..."

"Hey, come on..."

"Why is it now suddenly so boring? What does that mean? What? As if he's fun all the time. He's funny on TV. And he's funny for my mom—that's sure an achievement. But none of that's funny for me. That's *boring* for me."

"Okay," I said to her, "this happens... A crisis."

A young guy with a shaved head overheard and leered in my face. I turned the other way. Two more stops. I moved to the very back of the tram and watched the rails leading away toward the city center.

"I don't know," she said.

"Come on, you'll sort it out."

"I don't know... Oh, go to fucking hell."

She didn't say that to me but, kind of, to him. Then she started to cry and hung up.

I looked through that rear window. I realized that everything is in motion, nothing is secure.

When I got home, I called her. We talked for a long time.

It was all still a mystery to me. I'd kind of got used to them being together. It's strange because later, when you look, sometimes you don't know why people were together. But while they're together you always think: that's them. You see them as a kind of twin-pack, and you're amazed when the box falls apart. That happens to me every time, as if I'm sort of naïve.

She was not planning to call him.

She said he'd have to win her all over again; he'd have to start fresh. Because he wasn't the same person.

And so nothing came of it.

I mean, I knew she loved him. She stood by him all those years. Because the change came over him quite abruptly, and before you wouldn't have guessed.

Still, I thought he'd call her. Or something like that.

And then guess what happened next: before a month had passed, Karlo started going with Sena X.

I certainly didn't expect that. We were all surprised. No one believed that he rated so highly. I mean, it's not that . . . But, kinda, she is Sena X, after all. You can say what you like, but everyone knows who she is.

Like, it wouldn't be strange for her to be going with a tycoon or some . . . I don't know . . . imposing businessman, or a crime boss. I mean, Karlo isn't swimming in cash, right? And then she turns out to be kind of okay. As if she's a normal girl after all. Everyone was a bit taken aback.

It's strange, like real and unreal at the same time. Take that evening when I arranged to meet Sara. I mean, I persuaded her to go out so she could take her mind off things a bit and not mope around at home forever. The gang agreed to meet at the club. So the two of us went there. She looked good. And everything was fine for a while, but at one point Čombe, who was sitting next to me, told me Karlo was coming.

"He just called me," he said. "He's on his way here."

"With *her*?" I asked.

"I guess."

I didn't tell Sara. Maybe I should have.

So she and I sat there, and a few minutes later I saw them come in. Sena X: kind of tastefully made up, in a sort of blazer, nothing glamorous. You wouldn't think it was her at first glance.

They were with a buddy of his and a few others I didn't know. They probably came in two cars.

Sara pretended not to notice, but I saw she was seething inside. She stared in front of her.

Karlo looked over our way and gave me a quick nod.

Čombe, Nikola, and Lea were a bit restless because they were sitting with us, and they looked at me with pained *what-now* faces, and Sara kept her eyes to herself. A god-awful atmosphere. Everyone was itching to move.

Sara glanced at them and said, "Go and say hello, you can see he doesn't dare come here."

And they got up and went over to him.

Sara looked at me and said, "Did you know about this?"

"No, I had no idea. Really."

I made a face to say I was sorry.

"Shit!" she snorted, and glanced around to decide where best to go out.

I realized she couldn't leave now without being a picture of misery.

"Come on, don't worry," I said.

But I felt a pressure in the back of my head.

I had the impression that half the club was looking our way, I got that impression from the aborted glances whenever I turned around. Everyone seemed to be talking and looking at Sena X and Karlo, and then at us. I mean, at Sara. You sort of know the story line: Sara was the one he left. I was just an innocent bystander.

That's what I felt, but there's no logic to it at all.

Because I know Sara threw him out.

But ever since, when I talk about Sena X, because people are interested what she's like and if she's really empty-headed, everyone simply knows that Karlo broke up with my friend because of Sena X.

They know it. They just know. Could it be any different? That my friend threw him out of the apartment and that Sena X just happened to find him? Come off it!

While Sara and I sat there in the club, I almost had that impression myself.

The feeling simply appears in your head: that everything looks the way people think. I mean, you know it's not like that, but you've got it up there in parallel.

Was he perhaps already with Sena X when he said it was boring?

I reflected on that.

Nope, no way. If he had been with her he wouldn't have put on that little voice. He would definitely have become big-headed instead.

"You threw him out, full stop," I said to Sara as we were sitting there.

"Why do you say that?" she asked.

"Because it's the truth."

"I don't know where this is going," she said.

I thought deeply.

"It's not right for him to bring her here," I said. "It really isn't."

"Oh, he's free to," she snapped.

Sometimes you really don't know what to add.

I looked that way a bit and saw that Lea, Čombe, and Nikola were still there. They were laughing with Karlo. Sena X smiled insipidly.

Then I felt a hand on my shoulder.

Sara said, "Wanna join them? It's no problem, I need a change of scene anyhow."

"Hey," I said, "I came here with you and you're staying."

"Me and Karli breaking up doesn't mean he's your enemy."

That's what she used to call him, "Karli." I don't know why—no one else did. You know, a nickname from the relationship.

"Oh, forget it," I said.

"I know how curious you are," she said, forcing a smile.

She was actually serious, and that made me angry.

"Look, we're sitting here and that's that," I said.

And so we sat there. There's something in her that snaps shut, and sometimes you have to prize it open like a shell. Okay, it's hard to say what would be going through my mind if I were in her position. You really don't know what to say, and then you have a bundle of thoughts and also the worry that you mustn't look as if you're consoling her as if she were wretched. And then you realize what you're thinking is wrong, because why should she be wretched, I mean where does that word for her come from, there's no reason for it, she really isn't that. But I felt sorry for her all the same.

"I'm going to the toilet," she said. "I'll be straight back."

She was gone for quite a while.

I went to search for her.

I was angry at her as I walked around the club, looking. I had the impression that she'd gone. I mean, you have to check every part of the club, and there are nooks and crannies where you can bump into a person you know and stop for a while, but you know what it's like when you feel someone has gone. You don't know how you know it, but it's as if you can see in space. I thought about that as I moved through the club, as I entered the toilet and cast a glance in the mirror on the way.

Honestly, it got on my nerves. What a nuisance. As if I was to blame for the muddle. I went through to the stage, looked at the small bar, then went back on the other side of the large bar. Karlo was there with the others, and in passing I called out to Lea, "You've got nicely snagged," and she said, "For three minutes..."

I passed them all and arrived back to where Sara and I had been sitting. Two guys were now there at our table.

The more handsome of the two said, "Sorry, this was yours."

Casually, as if he knew me. The fellow had been sitting close by before, I had glanced at him, and he remembered that.

"No," I said, "I'm looking for my friend."

I looked around a little more, and he said, "Hey, who knows where she's gone, but we're here. Have a drink."

"No thanks," I said. "I'm here with them."

I headed for Karlo and the crowd.

When he introduced us and we both said "Pleased to meet you," I looked back at that guy. He was staring dumbfounded at Sena X. He had probably only noticed her now. I waited for him to return his eyes to me so I could snub him.

Just imagine falling in love with a loser like that.

On the Border

EVERY FEW DAYS he would find his rowboat on the other side of the river. Going and bringing it back was not so simple. Somewhere in his head, in a small afterthought, the moving of the boat to the other bank began to resemble a *sign* for him.

He was on watch for the fifth night in a row. He was not used to sleeping during the day, it was poor sleep and he was already very tired, but he had committed to seven nights, and he would see it through. Then he would sleep for as long as he needed to recover. But he knew he would be unnerved if he found the boat had been moved when he ended his watch. If someone was going to come, let them come now. Even if it was all a sign, let it come now.

His eyes were falling shut, so he decided to go for a short walk to clear his mind. Walking slowly, he could hear the river: a soft murmur that was lost during the day. Then he leaned his back against a slanting tree trunk. Its roots stuck out and its branches touched the water. Soon it would be carried away by the river.

The night was so acoustic, he thought. *For orchestra*. A crescent moon. Imagine an orchestra, the cheeks of the brass players, and the swift movements of the conductor beneath the moon. He felt he could hear them.

He felt he could hear someone. A distant whisper, which seemed to come through time. A wisp of mist clinging to the surface of the river. He no longer knew how old he was. He had been a boy when they whispered by the river, long, long ago, before the fighting.

The mist traveled, wafting past him, occasionally enveloping him. Something moved, he thought. Shadows.

Let it come now.

He took several steps toward the boat and bent down in front of the bushes, which he knew well. He went into the bushes a few yards from the boat. He sat down silently on a stool he had put there when he began his watch. A cocked pistol in one hand and a flashlight in the other.

He heard whispering that the river brought from upstream. So I'm not imagining it, he thought.

He heard a rustling. He waited, looking into the black like a cat, and finally he saw it. No, he was not imagining: some creature went up to the boat, sniffling. He did not get up or show himself, but only pointed the pistol and shouted, "Stop! Hands up!"

There came a muffled hubbub, like from a brood of animals. The commotion stirred fear in him. When he appeared in front of them pointing his pistol, shouting again with all his heart— "Hands Up! Give yourself up!"—they stood in the flashlight's beam like startled rabbits.

At first he could not see them, the eyes need a minute to adjust. He heard a female voice, which surprised him. Then he saw that young woman: black-haired, dark-eyed, beautiful.

For an instant his vision blurred, he felt a twitch of pain in his shoulder, and he staggered a little, but he remained on his feet. He thought something had hit him, so he shone the flashlight

ROBERT PERIŠIĆ

on himself and looked at his shoulder, chest. At the same time he issued a muted snarl: "Don't move an inch!"

They stood in horror: an apparition, as gaunt as a mummy, had emerged from the darkness and was now illuminating itself and murmuring incomprehensibly—is that how he looked to them?

It's fine, he thought. No blood, nothing. Maybe some nerve had given him a jab. And to think he had almost pulled the trigger. The thought made him break out in a sweat.

"Who are you?" he shouted so they would not think he was frail.

He counted them. There were five.

He saw one small, gray man speak some words, fold his hands imploringly, and hold his arms up to the sky.

He was angry.

They sat in his house on the floor, in the corner.

He gave them some food, but he did not put down his pistol.

Where were they heading?

He did not recognize the language they spoke. In his nine decades he had never heard such a hodgepodge of tones and he realized they were from far away and their journey had been long.

He was angry, not knowing what to do with them. He had thought everything would be over when he caught them red-handed. He did not expect they would sit in his house and murmur in their faraway language, casting glances at him as if they saw he was a good man. It got on his nerves even more the way they kept looking at him as if he was a little old man, as if their fear from the beginning had entirely left them.

He was drowsy, his eyelids stuck together, he could barely see them. What would happen if he fell asleep? Would they tie him up and rob him? They did not look dangerous, but he knew they would not be so foolish as to look dangerous. Once he had been a captive himself and behaved accordingly, until his moment came. The lad, who might have been a brother of the dark-eyed woman, seemed just a boy, but you never know.

He got up and scowled at them, one after another, to keep them on edge. They looked like a lost family, he thought. The dark-eyed woman replied with an almost impudent gaze. As if to say: go on, do it, call the police.

He felt his whole body tremble, and that pain in his shoulder returned. He sat down again on his chair and swore. He watched them and his eyes stung from lack of sleep. He was angry at them because he already knew. As he sank into sleep he knew he had to go across the river.

He saw himself plying the river at the crack of dawn.

He saw them wave from the other bank, into the dawn that resembled twilight because the sun had turned, and it is different from the western side.

ROBERT PERIŠIĆ

The Grande Finale

IT WAS THE grand finale.

I was sitting in shorts and a T-shirt. From there I watched him remove his belt, then he crouched down and measured. Shook his head. Nodded.

He's good.

Everybody says so. My father's good.

Perhaps the best.

Competitors poured in from all corners of the world. Quite a few came from the north: from Zagreb, and all the way from Hamburg and Stockholm. One even came from New York.

They have no idea.

They live in those cities like the blind. When they come here they want to prove something, and win.

They play in halls and pay membership fees. They play with top-quality balls.

But my father knows every speck of gravel in the court. And he can't stand that word, "balls."

"Them and their fuckin' 'balls,' he says. "Can't they say 'boules'?"

He plays with boules, very old boules, which maybe I'll inherit. If I get back on track.

That's what he said once.

I almost laughed at the extent to which he doesn't see me, at how obstinate he is about that.

Inheriting. Maybe. If.

Those boules.

Yes. That's one of the things that gives me a motive to live.

I watched him put on his belt and adjust his trousers.

I saw it on his face. What had happened the year before was a pure coincidence. He waited for them to come, and they came: amateurs.

Fifty or so people were now watching attentively. And twice that many came to chat and see in passing who would win the lamb on the spit and fifty liters of wine.

There was also a traveling trophy in the shape of a boule on a stand, the work of a local hobbyist sculptor.

But heavy clouds came up from behind the Mosor range and there was a change of weather.

He raised his head and looked. I listened. There was a rattle up on the awning. I took off my sunglasses. Yep. A rain shower began.

Like in Wimbledon.

My old man spread his arms.

Then he came up gradually. He walked broad-legged, with his belly out. He had an issue with his hips, as if they were separated.

They sat down at the next table.

He said to me, "What's up? Bored?"

"No," I said. "Did you two win?"

"Just one more point," he said.

"Ivanka!" he yelled. "Ivanka, bring him another beer, and us too!"

His pals were already sitting. They shook their heads and looked into the sky.

ROBERT PERIŠIĆ

The four of them. The finalists. An Andro from Zagreb and a Stipe from Hamburg, against Marinko, who lives in Split, and my father, who never goes anywhere.

The tension was postponed and the anticipation grew. This was the climax of the season.

Finally, Krama arrived through the rain, carrying his goggles and flippers under one arm.

The awning was broad, but the wind carried the droplets far inside. Water ran down the sides.

Krama came to the table in his Union Jack swim trunks and said, "What? You ain't moved an inch!"

"No," I said. "Where would I go?"

"To the beach, fuck it!" Krama enthused. "It's awesome."

Not even the shower could put him off. He really enjoys things. I don't know why he likes it so much here, of all places. He came with me one time from Zagreb and simply fell in love, as he says. In this awesomeness—the sea, the smells, the people—they looked at him a bit strangely. With his goggles, snorkel, and flippers.

A grown man. With a lot of flab on his frame. That's Krama. Awesome.

We each ordered a beer. The rain had no intention of stopping.

Krama spread out on the chair, ran his hands through his wet hair, and said, "Fantastic."

Otherwise, the rest of the year, Krama sits in Zagreb pubs and complains that things are unbearable. He says we have talented people, but it's hicks and goons who prosper because the normal folk keep quiet. He says that all year. Periodically he falls into a critical delirium and claims that only scum walk the streets, that there are no talented people here at all, and that nobody is sane.

Then he comes here and says: fantastic.

I don't know what to talk about with him anymore.

I nodded toward the goggles. "Did you see anything special?"

"All sorts of things, man. There's a cove full of little fishes, and they don't even turn tail."

That's exactly what he said, "little fishes."

"And?"

"Nothin', I mean, I could watch 'em all day."

I sipped my beer.

From the next table, my old man glanced at me from time to time and then looked away again. We hardly ever talk. Except in front of other people. It's different in front of people. We don't have any problems.

"Ivanka!" he called. "Bring us a round 'ere! An' them two as well!"

Ivanka poured the beers and served them. The storm intensified.

I tried to play along with it all. I said cheers to him. Krama did too.

"Your old man's a cool dude," he said.

I just laughed.

"What? He isn't?"

"He wrecks pretty much every day for me."

Every time I come to visit, I psyche myself up; I've been to therapy, too.

I try not to be a child. I try to see it all from a distance. But it all comes back to me. It's as if I seize up and stiffen inside; after that there's nothing, only defense mechanisms.

Sometimes I try to talk: about it not being a threat if I speak, about there being forms of communication other than domination. But you can't, not in his house. Anxiety.

He's probably afraid of me taking control, even though I've moved out. I only want to see them; my mother more than him. He brings me down and this place is dark for me. I've been there a week, I just drink, and I'll have to leave so as to avoid any deeper immersion in a place without air. Best tomorrow. Then they'll wonder. Mother will be sad. He'll be angry. Because I'm bad. A bad son. I neglect them. And here I have the sea, the sun, everything. I consider how to explain that to someone, perhaps to Krama? But Krama is in awe. He watches the little fishes.

He and I try to outwit each other, that's our game, it's all fun.

"Krama," I said, "how about I go to Zagorje and watch the cows?"

"What? Cows?"

"How about I go to where you come from, go up to the cows, and stare. I think they deserve it."

"Whaddya mean?"

"It occurred to me that it's nice for you to watch the little fishes here, and maybe it'd be super for me to watch little cows. What's the difference? It's all nature."

"Nooo, no difference," Krama drawled sarcastically.

He smiled up his sleeve and finished his beer while he was coming up with something. I ordered him another.

"Then I'll walk around Zagorje, explaining to people how awesome it is. Don't the little cows deserve it? And the little calves are so cute."

"Go right ahead."

I thought what more to add.

We were used to the rain now.

My father was waving his arms at the next table. I pretended not to be listening. But, unbelievably, Marinko announced he had to go home to Split.

"Are you mad?" my father shouted.

Marinko said he couldn't wait for the storm to pass. He had to go, his wife had called him five times. His mother-in-law had been rushed to the hospital and they were keeping her there, and he had to go. His wife couldn't drive and he had to take her.

"You can win the point without me," Marinko told my old man.

My father cast a piercing glance at him. It also turned out that Marinko had won all their points so far. But it had nothing to do with the points. It was a matter of principle.

Marinko acted angry as he got up from the table, as if his day had been ruined. He paid for his drinks, cursed his rotten luck, and simply left. He dashed to his car, started it, turned on the lights and wipers.

My father's face clouded over. I saw he wasn't going to say anything, but he decided he would never forget that day.

My father stared blankly into the downpour.

"What now?" someone muttered.

"Marinko, that dickhead," hissed another voice.

"Steady on! The man's mother-in-law must really be dyin', otherwise 'e wouldn'ta gone."

Commotion.

"If she doesn't die, I don't want to hear from him anymore," Stipe from Hamburg said.

There was a laugh.

My old man looked around like an abandoned child. There was no denying it: the legendary duo had been split. They'd never play together again.

Krama sensed the depth of the situation. He ordered two more beers for us.

"How about you play?" he suggested.

I waved dismissively.

"Why not?"

"It's his thing."

"No, seriously. I don't get it, what . . ."

"Why should I play with him?"

He pressed me to imagine the scene: the two of us winning, winning together. But that wasn't something I wished for.

ROBERT PERIŠIĆ

Perhaps I'm a hard man too.

My mother sometimes tells me I'm just like him.

Why can't you give in a bit, she says.

We both treat her the same way, she says.

We only ever think of ourselves, she says.

I'd love to find a way not to think about myself.

Mother reminds me that we should keep our shames *in the house* and I shouldn't talk about those sorts of things, at least not while I'm there. Nor about why I didn't come with Mirna, from whom she had been expecting a grandchild. Say that she couldn't get vacation, my mom suggested. Why does anyone have to know? And maybe you'll make up, she said. All right, Mom, everything's just perfect, we don't have any problems. Let it be like that just for today. Tomorrow I'll be saying my vacation has abruptly been cancelled. Today we'll talk your way. See, I'm giving in a bit. It's not true that I don't think of you.

Would it would mean something to her if he and I won together? It would certainly look good. I rushed down my beer. I felt the tension at the next table, all the looks and glances. The rain eased up.

Then Stipe from Hamburg turned and asked, "Wanna play?"

"Me?" I said.

"Yeah, who else?"

I glanced at my old man. He was staring away, glowering.

"There are better," I said.

The sun's rays broke through gaps in the clouds. Krama gave a stupid smile and nodded toward a rainbow. I saw it rather darkly.

"C'mon, just take the balls there so we can finish up," Stipe urged.

My old man was silent. He turned and looked at me as if he was gauging my personality once more.

I felt, at the end, that I saw something imploring in his eyes.

People began to get up and walk out to the playing area.

I stood up, cleared my throat, and said, "All right then."

I carried the boules. My father walked beside me.

Then he stopped and said, looking straight ahead, "I'll play the first two. We just need one point, understand? You mightn't even need to play."

I watched my old man throw the first, the way he balanced on one leg, twisted in the air, and slowly extended his right arm in the desired direction, as if trying to influence the course of the boule, which was already rolling. It trundled along, passed Andro's, made a gentle curve at the end, and came to rest right next to the jack.

My father didn't say a word to anybody. He just went, "Aha."

Then the other side threw their two boules.

Stipe from Hamburg held the last and concentrated.

I was hot and nervously peeled off my T-shirt.

Stipe took a run-up and threw forcefully. He knocked ours away.

"Good shot!" my father said.

Now they had three points, but we had three boules left. They had none. Winning was a must.

My old man threw. He balanced on one leg and made that famous figure of concentration on the distance. Then he ran there. He bent down and had a close look. He removed his belt. He and Stipe crouched down and measured. Everyone gathered around. Old Marin, who was up close, gestured to me that my father had won, and that I could throw the boules down in front of me.

I just had to drop them to the ground.

That was all of my game, my contribution to the victory.

But as he was getting up from his haunches after taking the measurements, the moment he looked at me to confirm that— my boule was in the air.

I watched it fly, I felt his eyes among all the others.

I heard a forceful "No!" in the air.

But the boule flew, fell, and rolled.

I made a movement with my body as if I was steering it remotely. I stopped, aslant.

It was going well, it was going brilliantly.

But one of theirs, completely away from where I was aiming, seemed to be in its path.

Would it pass by, or touch it?

It touched it.

I grasped my temples.

Amazingly, their boule knocked away my father's and now stood there, closest to the jack. I had to correct that immediately, before he had the opportunity to say anything, so I threw my second boule, I heard people's murmur, it came sailing in with a fury and changed everything, which is what I wanted: it struck the jack, reconfigured the whole situation, and now it was just a question of luck where it would stop.

I couldn't see exactly from where I was.

My father crouched down. Then he knelt. Then he bent over at the middle.

There was a lot of noise there, a lot of voices. His wasn't the strongest, and he didn't shout, but somewhere among all the other voices, from deep inside, it stood out among all the others.

"People ... I have a son ... I have a son ... A hopeless boozer."

He said it again. And kept on repeating it.

I watched from this side of the court, like from a stage.

His voice became stronger. As if he was calling for help in front of all the people.

I saw them. I saw Krama among them. He was holding his goggles, snorkel, and flippers and watching me from there.

My old man got up.

I felt I would fall. But it had nothing to do with the beer. Nothing at all.

He took his boules and left for the waterfront. He was still repeating those stupid words.

He threw one boule into the sea with all his strength.

Did he really throw it into the sea?

Now he threw the second one and hit someone's yacht. I heard the blow but didn't see exactly where it landed.

The people moved apart. But I ran there and flung myself into the water. I swam to the yacht. There I saw it, on the deck. Then I swam to where the first one sank.

Now I'm there somewhere.

I look back toward the shore to gauge the right location. I see people at the waterfront, in a blur, for an instant I hear voices, and then water.

I'm looking at the sea from within.

I look at the bottom and go down to it. I search. I can't see it. I roam the bottom.

How long has it been already, do I still have air?

All that pressure, down in my insides. The drumming silence.

Distortion. Strange colors.

"You can't see me," it whispers.

Where is it?

Something dark over there. Is that it? No, it's coming toward me. It's not close, but it's coming. Approaching. Little fishes. An enormous school of them. And they pass through, for ages and ages.

I Emerged Somewhere Else

THERE ARE CIGARETTE butts shoved into the sand around my towel, two crunched up beer cans. The criminal who had evaded justice calmly stares back at me from the newspaper headlines. Domestic folk music comes from the outdoor patio of a nearby café.

I'm pale.

From behind dark sunglasses, I watch two gorgeous girls playing picigin with boys.

All those sparkling dots of light.

I've been sitting on this beach like a dog tied up in the sun.

I lay down and squint up at the sky.

Tanning.

Forty-five minutes have passed.

The sea is mainstream. Everyone goes in, like in a club.

The sea is commercial.

Am I going to burn?

I sit up and light a cigarette. Boys are jumping around like crazy in the shallow water and the girls catch their balance while their tits bounce around.

I pull my watch out of my shoe. Okay, one more swim.

I get up and walk into the sea for the last time, like a fake suicide attempt.

My feet slowly search for the bottom, I keep going, then pull my legs up, my face hits the water, I leave public life. It's not like anyone here knows me anymore anyway.

I'm swimming, for quite some time already.

I go out a little further. I want to see how far I can go. I can probably swim the length of a football pitch.

And I've had enough. I flip onto my back, floating like that in the water, and look up.

I'm breathing as if I've been punctured. Am I able to make it back?

"Heeey," a voice echoes.

I raise my head and, even though it doesn't make sense, water rushes into my mouth.

Then I see a face.

I think to myself, that voice and those big, bloody eyes.

No, it can't be.

It's gotta be a flashback.

I dip beneath the surface, to clear my head. Old conversations start coming back to me: This too shall pass . . . we love each other . . . the war can't do anything to us . . .

I come up for air and she's still there. I wanted to say, "Oh, how did I get here?"

I wanted to shout: "You have to understand, I didn't know what to do with all those letters. The city-wide blackouts fucked me up, I couldn't plan anymore. The POW exchanges fucked me up, I wanted to run away, but instead I just stayed, and stayed." You know that feeling of staying behind, in some hole in the wall, in the big city, in that life that unexpectedly drags on.

But now, I was waving my arms soundlessly beneath the water, saying: "Hey, what are you doing here?"

The pointlessness of that question usually goes unnoticed, but when you run into someone at a depth of twenty feet, the pointlessness becomes apparent. It reverberates.

She smiles. "I came back. I'm here for good now."

Yeah, I think, catching my breath: here, she's here for good.

She floats around, waiting for me.

"How about you?" she says.

I wanted to push it out along with all the air from my lungs, those blinds dammit, those blinds were pulled all the way down, they didn't let any light in, total blackout, I was in a capsule, breathing rapidly, I wanted to explain, I ate canned food, on the ground floor, in the rented kitchen, with white tiles on the floors and walls, the faucet stuck out from the middle of the wall, above it was a cupboard, beneath it was the bed, but it wasn't safe, that's what they said on the radio, so I pushed the bed all the way over to the door, and I didn't know what to do, I couldn't do anything anymore, and these letters would come every day, the letters would start, and as soon as they would begin, I would sink deeper and deeper, thinking nobody really knows me. I was just waving my arms in place.

The letter read: My love, it's almost midnight. I'm thinking about you.

She wrote that. After she already went across the border.

How about you?

Me, yes me, I'm keeping my head above water and now we're ten feet apart. My wartime love, her bloody eyes, they're coming this way.

She's coming over to me, and what now? Maybe a handshake?

No, there's no shaking hands in the water.

Maybe a kiss on one cheek and then the other?

I don't know how you're supposed to greet someone in the water. She stops. And now maybe, if I get closer, if I graze her back with my hand, and if our legs bump together, no, it can't be: all that shine, memories from the beginning of the war and little white dots, sun in my eyes, sex and fear, breathing, doggy paddling and doggy style, water in our mouths and cum on wet, white sheets. I pause mid-stroke, staying there panting because I'm scared, and I raise my hand for a moment, waving, as if this is an official goodbye, because we never had one of those.

I didn't know what to do with all those letters, I sink further down, far away shouts from the beach, a commotion, waves of voices.

I say, "So, I dropped by..."

She looks at me, as if to say, "I'm doing fine here and I'm getting used to it. I found a job, not an official one of course, they pay me under the table. But my life is still connected to yours and to my home, my only one. I constantly think about you and Croatia."

How strange.

I catch my breath and ask, "How are you?"

I wanted to say, imagine, those letters were coming every day, but... But yea, we're still here, in reality, keeping our heads above water. We're managing that much, just like you.

She says, breathing through her mouth, "I'm fine. How about you?"

I wave my arms around in the water, at a distance.

Spitting seawater out of my mouth, I say, "Everything's fine."

She looks at me, as if to say it's raining.

Her body shimmers, all wavy in the water. I try to take a good look.

A sound barrier.

"What did you say?" I ask.

Early morning, we're going to a protest in some town.

I barely keep my head above water. And I see how I'm lying inside a cloud of smoke, smoking York cigarettes, my skin is all broken out from eating too much canned food, I'm reading something, but I can't make any sense of it, sounds are floating in the ether, I turn off the radio, then on again... This is ground control to Major Tom... Your circuit's dead, there's something wrong. Can you hear me Major Tom... Can you heee... My arms hurt.

"How about you?"

"I didn't hear you," I say.

"You. Everything still same old, same old?" she asks. With a bit of a grin.

People who don't believe in me anymore ask like that.

But nothing is the same. It seems to me that her face is twisted into a permanent grimace and that she's aged in a bad way. My neck muscles tense up and start to hurt.

"I'm going back, I'm gonna drown."

"Me too," she says, gulping in air.

I look at her. It's as if her head has been severed with light. Fresh, still wet watercolor. I turn around.

I stare at those letters. Someone was inviting someone else to come.

It's nice here and you'll like it.

I was distancing myself.

All that's left is an empty feeling of powerlessness and thoughts preoccupied mostly with you.

I swim, barely.

Finally I reach shore, touch the bottom.

I look all around. I don't see her. I don't know where she is.

I come out of the water. My body's tense. I feel every muscle. The sand is hot. I start walking so I can sit down and think.

But my stuff wasn't there.

I stare at an empty spot and then it all makes sense to me, as if I was ready for it.

My stuff wasn't there. No newspaper, no cans, no cigarette butts.

There were no traces at all.

I lower my head and sit down like that because, I don't know why, I start to worry that people might figure me out.

I sit there and act like everything's okay.

Some time passes and then I see it. Yes. It's simple. I emerged somewhere else.

It's fine, I see: my things are over there, a little further away.

I look over at them, from where I'm sitting.

All I have to do is go to them.

Translated by CHELSEA SANDERS

ROBERT PERIŠIĆ

Hey, Joe

JOE WAS PUTTING the caps on the ice cream cones. The conveyor belt rattled. He tried to think of something else. He tried to loosen up. Then one of the managers came in and clapped twice. Joe looked at those hands.

"The boss is coming," the manager shouted, surveying the scene. "Work normally, unless he asks you something."

The manager's hands slowly fell down beside his body, like he was a conductor.

Joe watched those hands falling. Then he turned back. The machines were working. Quiet or loud, it's hard to say, depends what you're used to.

A worker who was hard of hearing repeated, "The boss is coming."

Then the manager left, slamming the door. Probably went into the yard to welcome the boss with the other honchos. The door was always being banged. As if that's what it was for.

The windows high up. Ashen light through the long hall. Particles of dust in the air. A few shadows ran. Workers stacked boxes, one on top of the other, climbed up on that structure like a rampart and looked out through the dirty panes.

Joe tried to think of something else. The individually-packed ice cream cones traveled along the belt toward him. He tried to loosen up. He knew quite a bit about the boss. While Joe had the Serbs on his mind, the guy bought this place for cheap. Joe had followed the affairs in the newspapers, and he still followed the "Life" section, studied the photos. That's how you get to see what life is.

The guy had a daughter who married in a wedding dress with an open back.

Joe was putting the caps on a batch of vanilla. He couldn't smell it. Or it didn't have a smell in the first place. It was just sticky. He put on the last cap.

The ice cream cones stopped traveling toward him. A bottleneck somewhere. He took out a cigarette and lit up. His team crowded around the windows. Dark shadows in front of the light from the east. Smoke in the air. Everything ran idle.

Somebody bit into a frozen treat, although it wasn't hot.

They waited for the boss. Each and every one of them would kill him, under certain circumstances, in their dreams.

Somebody yelled, "Here he is!"

Joe went and climbed up onto the boxes too. He stared through the dirty glass smudged by Zagreb's rain and soot. Three big black BMWs crept into the courtyard, quietly, like giant cats. Only without the teeth, but Joe had a feeling they were there somewhere. Ten of them or so in dark suits, with ties, got out of the Beamers.

All of that seemed to sharpen the picture.

Outside, old Jura and his team were fixing something. They were handing it back and forth to one another. Then they'd gather round and inspect it. It looked as if they were performing a sketch.

Joe saw through the owner straightaway. After shaking hands with the managers he approached Jura's team. He said something to them and then stared at what they were looking at. Jura

ROBERT PERIŠIĆ

replied, spreading his arms slightly, and the boss nodded and made a quip. Then he said something serious. You could tell, the guy was a smooth talker. He always asked nicely and spoke nicely, like a news anchorman.

The workers muttered:

"What can you do?"

"That's how it is."

"Could be worse."

"It's not bad."

"It's okay."

Joe got down from the rampart of boxes, crushed out his cigarette, went back to the conveyor belt, and called, "Hey, workin' class! Where are the ice creams?"

"What's up?"

"C'mon, c'mon!"

He put on the caps. The same as before. He put them on all the time. But when he saw the managers come in with the owner ten minutes later, Joe strolled to a bench by the wall, stretched, and sat down.

It's time, he thought. He looked around the hall. He caught a few astonished glances in that forest of machines and overalls. He'd decided. He couldn't allow that smoothy to ask him something in passing. After all, Joe had once been a rebel of sorts. He didn't care—let them sack him. He lay down on the bench, put an arm under his head, and shut his eyes. He stayed like that for a while.

Beyond his eyelids the humming of the machines seemed to have intensified. A gaggle of voices appeared and then receded into a crackling and buzzing, like when you search for a distant station on the radio because you no longer trust the ones you can hear well. Joe now waited on that obscure frequency. He awaited the outcome there in his darkness.

The boss should turn up any minute now and say, "What's he doing here?"

Joe decided it all in an instant. He hadn't planned what he was going to say. But he knew he had to say something. Something god-fucking awesome that would be told and retold in the factory even when people had forgotten what he looked like, where he came from, who he was, and if that famous guy, Joe, even existed at all. He needed something that would be remembered until the last ice cream came off the belt, until people thought up something else to eat when they wanted to cool off their tongues.

"What's he doing here?"

Maybe he should open his eyes and say, "None of your fucking business."

No, that's old hat.

Maybe, "Your mansion suits me fine, thank you."

No, what's that got to do with it?

Maybe, "I'm waiting for all this to pass."

Nah, no oomph.

Maybe, "My blood pressure's gone through the floor. Can you get me a coffee?"

That's Šurda, from the Yugoslav TV series *Hot Wind*. It's not bad, but something original would be better.

Or just say, "I'm Joe" and reach out his hand?

Yes, yes, it was about who he was, what he did, what made him what he was.

Because sometimes, recently, it had seemed to him, in an insidious way, that he was no longer himself, which vexed him severely, and he would get sloshed without a trace of mirth. But now, as he lay there, he felt again like he had before, he was quite sure he was his old self again. Good old Joe. That cheered him up him so much that he almost laughed. Really, perhaps he should just say, "Joe is Joe again!" No, nobody would get it.

ROBERT PERIŠIĆ

Loads of possible answers passed through his head from second to second and he arranged them automatically like mail is sorted. Once he worked in a post office and he knew what that looks like, and this looked like the same process, performed by a hundred staff at the same time: *whiz, whiz, whiz, whiz, whiz*. He felt his brain humming louder than all those Swedish packaging machines and he remembered the stories where a person experiences clinical death and sees their whole life in a flashback. That's just how he felt, so it occurred to him that he could say to the boss, when he finally came and asked what he was doing, "I was clinically dead!"

He felt like an eternity had passed since he shut his eyes. Then he realized it had probably only been a minute or two, and he went on waiting. I'm here, you poor bastards, he spoke inside, feeling like he was living inside that song. Look over here. Farewell, cockroaches!

Later, he decided to open his left eye a little: it quivered. He saw the ceiling shake in a blur, and he heard the monotonous humming. He lowered his eyelid again.

He waited.

Later, when he opened his eyes and raised his head, he saw they were already far away, at the other end of the hall. He propped himself up on his elbows. He simply couldn't see the boss, nor the boss him, because the managers had positioned themselves to block the guy's view in Joe's direction.

He thought, Man, what now?

The boss stayed in that position for a time. Then they went out through the far door. The manager went last and didn't slam it.

Joe thought it was stupid to lie there. He got up and went back to his place. He felt eyes on him, and he stared at the traveling ice cream cones.

He stood like that for a time. Then he started to put on the caps.

When the manager came later, all flushed, he said, "I was sweating blood and water."

Joe didn't act innocent and ask why that was, otherwise he probably would have been sacked.

The manager bridled his rage and said mockingly, "Think you deserve a damn medal?"

Joe didn't know if the manager was afraid of him or even liked him. The guy was a big-time crook and black-marketeer. Once, they said, he also worked on the line. Perhaps he feared Joe could say some of the things he'd heard. Perhaps he kind of respected Joe's unruliness because he considered himself unruly as well. He had been a real heavy once. He didn't have an education. Maybe he had some plans for Joe, maybe he thought they were the same, and he was just older and more experienced.

He raised his finger and said, "I'll forgive you this one last time—because it's you."

Joe could have up and said, "Who asked for forgiveness?" But he didn't. He'd lost the urge.

He should have been an actor.

Afterward everyone talked about how Joe pretended to be asleep.

They say he's a real hardcore rebel who's ashamed to be doing what he's doing. It could ruin his reputation. What would his gang say if they found out he slaves away here?

His coworkers call him "the actor," and now he's very popular.

And really, he could have starred in some cool movie. Joe wanted to become an actor, but he never did a thing. He just hung around for a while in some theater pubs. It didn't work out.

Besides, our domestic movies are crap.

They don't exist.

ROBERT PERIŠIĆ

Who cares about them?

Joe puts the caps on ice cream cones. It's also a movie. The conveyor belt. His room. Chow. Beer. TV.

Three Legs

I THINK IT was the last time I saw him.

Wait. Did we see each other again after that?

No, it can't have been the last time we met, because we were waiting for the ferry that ran when the Maslenica Bridge was down.

We saw each other after that. I'm wrong about that being the last time.

I was basically waiting for the ferry, and he stayed. He sat with me so I wouldn't have to wait alone. Its departure was delayed and we talked for a long time, which is no small thing, and drank together. Some cow was constantly mooing. I looked to see where it was coming from and saw a truck that was transporting cattle. The livestock was packed in tight and one cow's lower leg was stuck in the railings of the truck between two partition boards.

It probably wanted to get away but got stuck instead, I reflected years later.

What did he and I talk about? There was something, I know. It wasn't said directly but was in the tone of the conversation, and the gist was that everything between us could be better.

Who knows why that stands out today, among all the others, as our last meeting.

Neither of us did anything.

No God in Susedgrad

DANKO GOT MARRIED and had a kid. Fantom and I hadn't seen him for months.

We'd given him a firm promise that we'd visit him in Susedgrad.

"We oughta go and see Danko, else he'll be angry," we often said.

That day we met in town, as usual. I didn't exactly have much dough. At least, not enough for me and Fantom, because he didn't have any. He drank at others' expense. He had a talent for scrounging and honed it to perfection. People paid for his drinks as if they felt obliged. He became legend.

But there was nobody anywhere. It was a Monday afternoon in the fall.

"Shall we go and see Danko?" I suggested.

After huffing and puffing about needing to take a tram and then a bus to get there, we set off.

"I've never been out to Susedgrad," Fantom said.

"Me neither."

We made it there and found his building, no problem. We climbed the stairs.

"Fuck, what do you think if he's not home, and we've come all this way," Fantom said.

We knocked, rang, and waited. He wasn't home.

I had the number of one of his relatives. He was always at home, Danko had said.

As we were leaving the building a woman was getting out of a Renault 5. It was just getting dark. Fantom asked where we might find a phone booth. We were far from having mobiles.

She started to give us directions. It turned out we were also far from any phone booth. The woman was pushing fifty but well-preserved. Plus well-to-do, you could see.

Fantom was depressed by the distance to the phone.

The woman laughed and asked, "Who are you looking for?"

We told her.

"You can phone from my place, if you like," she said.

We climbed the stairs after her. She was on the second floor. Fantom winked at me, like, the old girl was his type.

We entered the apartment. There was barking.

"Just a minute and I'll shut him in," the lady said.

But a big boxer headed toward us. Fortunately, the lady caught him by the collar. She dragged him into the room, while he tried to dig in with his hind legs. She'll throttle him, I thought. The boxer scraped over the parquet, growling and staring at us with bulbous eyes. The lady closed the door, and the boxer was on the other side.

"Where's your phone?" I asked.

She pointed. It was in front of my nose.

I hastily dialed the number. The boxer barked and pounded against the door. Fantom launched into talking about how lovely the apartment was. The lady was kind and smiley. I got a connection. The boxer was scratching at the door. The lady disappeared somewhere. I thought she was putting on coffee. The phone rang, there at Danko's relative's place. Nobody answered. The boxer leaned on the doorknob. The door opened and the boxer's head popped out.

"Missus!" I yelled.

Fortunately she was already there. She squeezed the animal back in. The dog growled and barked behind the frosted glass. Then she went back to the kitchen.

I hung up.

"Thanks," I called out and backed toward the door, with Fantom following. We pushed one another out and rushed down the stairs.

We were some way from the building when we dared to speak.

"What a dog, man."

Buildings dotted the fields. It was dark and chilly.

We searched for the town center. We asked some kids with bags. The center, or at least a bar. We found a bar. Sat down with a beer.

"We sure arc heroes," I said.

We laughed at ourselves.

"How about the old girl," Fantom said wistfully. "Man, I'd screw her on the spot!"

He was always ridiculous when he was serious.

"If we hadn't scatted she might've offered us coffee."

"Or tea."

"I think she was about to," he said.

"She's got dough," I added.

"We should try and tickle some out of her. Then we'd all have it good."

Fantom had always wanted to be a gigolo.

"Shit, it's too late now," I said.

"Man, maybe she'd be up for a threesome. The old girl's progressive, hundred percent. She does her own thing, she's got the itch!"

"Come off it."

"Why should you care? Party pooper!" he said.

I took a sip of beer and held my tongue.

"Let's go back, who gives a fuckin' damn!"

"Come off it, who wants to go all the way back there?"

Fantom insisted. I had cold feet. The whole plan was pretty damn stupid. But I didn't want be a wet blanket. We finished our beers and set off.

"What'll you say to her?" I asked.

"Nothin' in particular. Like, we've come to use the phone again. We'll see how she reacts."

"Listen, if you wanna screw her—go ahead. I'll mind the door," I said. "I don't think I'd ever get hard with that dog around."

"Oh, come on, man, she'll lock it in," Fantom said.

We approached her door. I stayed a few steps behind, for safety. Fantom tapped his nose and rang. Silence. The dog didn't bark. I had a feeling the lady was looking through the peephole and thinking. Then we heard the key turn in the lock. The door opened. An elderly, well-nourished beardo stood in the doorway.

Fantom stared at him.

"Yes?" the guy said.

He probably didn't see me, and I drew back behind the corner of the stairway.

Fantom said nothing at first. Then he said sheepishly, "The lady?"

"Who are you?"

"A friend," Fantom said.

I had drawn back deep into my cover. Then I saw Fantom come flying down the stairs. I started after him. He was running like mad. We rushed out of the building and around behind it, stomped through some mud, and found ourselves on a road full of puddles. I was convinced they were searching for us. There was an old shack there. We snuck beneath the eaves, into the dark. I leaned against the wall and caught my breath.

"What happened?"

"Nothin'. He looked at me a bit, and went to get her. Then I bolted."

"Oh, fuck," I said and started to laugh.

Fantom also gave a helpless laugh.

When he got serious he reflected, "Man, that guy'll bust her up!"

"What a slob," I said.

"You bet. Man, he'll beat the livin' daylights out of her."

"What now?"

"Opportunity wasted," Fantom sighed.

"Fuck . . . and the woman was okay. I mean, she didn't even know us."

"It was a mistake," Fantom said. "Whoever helps me gets screwed."

It looked as if he really regretted it.

My laughter evaporated. Fantom's conscience came alive. After so many years.

I lit a cigarette. He took one too.

"Fuckin' hell, we really are trash," he said.

He gave a maudlin smile and gazed at the moon. We stood there like that and smoked. I looked back at the building. The upper stories could be seen. It seemed to me that a light was now on in Danko's apartment. I wanted to tell Fantom.

Oohoo . . .

"What the fuck?"

The muted voice came from inside the shack. I didn't think anybody lived there, but something began to scrape in the dark behind us. A door opened with a creak. Every hair on my body stood on end.

Maybe we could have waited to see what it was. But now we were in the mud again. We slogged through shit and puddles, looking over our shoulders, and made it back to the building. I headed for the entrance.

"C'mon," I said to Fantom, pulling him by the sleeve. He resisted. I told him I'd seen a light.

"I'm not goin' in, dead or alive," he said.

We pressed up against the side of the building as if poised for a guerilla attack.

We'd survived the war, but now we were in a funk. There was no way out in Susedgrad! One fucking hitch after another.

"The guy didn't see me," I said.

I wanted to be inside, in Danko's fucking apartment, to see his wife and child. He invited us, fucking hell!

"I'm gonna try it out, and I'll send Danko to get you," I proposed.

"I'll go there for a while," Fantom said, pointing in a vague direction. "See that post?"

"Yeah."

A lamp was shining on top of it. It was about a hundred yards away.

"I'll be there, a bit around the other side," Fantom said as if he was going to the front line.

And he was off. I entered the building, climbed the stairs, and went up to the lady's door. It was deathly quiet. I put my ear to the door, but nothing was to be heard inside. Then the dog started barking. I leaped several steps at a time—fourth, fifth, sixth floor—and arrived at Danko's door. Somebody further down turned on the light. I rang and didn't take my finger off the buzzer.

A woman opened.

"I'm a friend of your husband's," I whispered, out of breath.

"Aha," she said without a smile.

Not to be put off, I rushed inside and shut the door.

"Don't worry," I puffed. "I'm just bein' chased by a dog!"

ROBERT PERIŠIĆ

"A dog?" she stared at me, looking like she was going to chuck me out.

"A very nasty dog." I leaned my back against the door.

Now she watched me with a trace of fear. She recoiled a step or two, and her whole body shuddered in a kind of sob.

I tried to calm things. "Y'know, we've come from Zagreb to see your kid and some dog scared the shit out of us."

That seemed to work. She called out to Danko. He was in the bathroom. She banged on the door.

"One of *your* friends is here!" she yelled.

She shot daggers from the corner of her eye and turned her back to me. I couldn't figure out if she was apprehensive or simply didn't want to have anything to do with me.

"That's the last fuckin' thing I need!" I heard him from behind the door.

I got the impression they were pretty pissed off at one another.

I walked into the kitchen and sat down. My eyes fell on my shoes. They were muddy. My trousers too, filthy up to the knees. Now she stared at the muddy trail I'd left behind me.

"Jesus!" she exclaimed.

"It was freakish, what was after us," I said with a pathetic smile.

"So there are several of you?" she asked. She was holding a coffeepot and looking into it with her head lowered. Then she raised her eyes.

"There's one more . . . buddy," I said kind of apologetically.

She just looked at me.

Never in my life had I felt anything like this: she stood there and watched me as a final confirmation that life was shit. As if I was just the dot on the *i* for her.

She probably wasn't satisfied with Danko, I thought. And seeing me here now, it all became clear to her. I had that feeling.

"Well, this is a strange situation," I said.

She didn't answer. She smiled a kind of ironic smile, staring now at me, now at the empty coffeepot. Like, no, it can't be, it's not possible.

I pretended to be looking about the apartment. It was clear that I'd gate-crashed at an awkward moment. Still, Danko's woman wasn't quite level, I thought. She looked at me as if I was a ghost. I pretended everything was all right, but a strange uncertainty crept into my mind. After the way things had started, I thought it could be a totally different Danko taking a bath. Oh, fuck, has anyone as much as mentioned the name?

Then I roused myself and looked at her. Who knows if it had been the right door. What did it say?

She caught my eyes. Yes, she sincerely hoped I wasn't her husband's friend. Where did he get friends like this?

I started to look around the apartment again. There ought to be a baby here somewhere. I felt like a plaything in somebody's hands. I was seriously fucked. Someone was severely messing me around. Just let it be Danko who comes out! If a completely unknown guy came out, I don't know... I was sick of everything. I had barged in, I thought. Where was the kid? There was no crying. I'd been to Danko's place by the Sava river a thousand times and he'd never been taking a bath when I came.

I thought of getting up and going. But I pretended everything was good. I thought of Fantom down beneath the lamppost. If the cops passed by they'd definitely pick him up.

I tried to broach a conversation while the coffee water was heating up and while that swine, whoever he was, was drying himself off, I assumed.

"How's the boy? Doesn't he cry?" I ventured.

As if surprised, she said, perplexed, "It's a girl. She's sleeping."

Where did I get the idea it was a boy? Did someone tell me that? If so... Then there was no way out. Part of my mind began

ROBERT PERIŠIĆ

to reconcile itself with that scenario. No one would be the one I was searching for. I'd never break out of this circle of misacquaintances. There was no way out of Susedgrad.

I thought of getting up. I should have fled back to Zagreb immediately, if Zagreb still existed. But I stayed sitting there, in Susedgrad.

I stared at the table in silence. The coffee water was boiling. The bathroom door opened. I didn't dare raise my eyes. Where did I get the bit about it being a boy? I browsed my fragmented memory. Then a hand thumped me on the back. I flinched with fright. I looked up.

Danko.

"What are you starin' at, huh?" He gave me a gentle clap on cheek.

"Nothin'."

"What's up, are you stoned?"

"I'm not, I swear!"

She looked behind him. Now she was sure. This was it. Her life was ruined.

"Are you trippin'? Why you gawkin' like that?" Danko behaved like an elder brother. It seemed he was making fun, but I saw he actually meant it.

I looked at him. There was nothing haywire, which gave some reason for hope.

"No, no," I said, "I'm as clean as a new pin, but Susedgrad. Fuck, it's like a house of horror.

"Oh?" she raised her eyebrows.

"I mean, that's just how it turned out."

"What happened?" he asked.

"Inexplicable! Call it Murphy's Law," I said. "Let's not go into it."

"Seen our little girl?" he said.

"No."

"Come have a look," he said, pointing to a door.

"Yep, just takin' off my shoes," I said.

He opened the door softly and led me into the dark room.

"Pssst," he went.

He took me a few steps through the dark. Now I had to look at the kid and say all the nicest things. We stood bending over a shadowy bundle in the dim light. I feared it would turn over and be a monster.

"That's her," he whispered.

"Aha, she's sleepin'."

"Sleepin'," he said too, but much more quietly.

"Let's go back," I whispered to him. "Fantom's waitin' outside under a lamppost."

"What?" he shouted.

Then the kid began to bawl. I left the room and said, "Fuck!" His wife went in. Now she'd get out her breast, I thought sadly.

I explained to Danko where Fantom was and that he should go and get him. He kept turning and looking in the direction of the screaming in the room. He was so absent that I had to explain everything to him several times over. He kept turning toward the room as if he was about to get up do something about it. I told him to go and get Fantom—there, at the lamppost. I repeated it three times.

"Don't you see the girl's cryin'!" he bellowed.

"Course I do!" I said, now sick to death of all of them.

He got up from his chair as if propelled by a spring.

"Fuckin' hell," he hissed. He paced up and down.

"What?" I asked.

"I'm sick of it! I'm so fuckin' sick of it all!" he snapped.

"What are you sick of?"

ROBERT PERIŠIĆ

"Oh, forget it," he said, waving dismissively. "Forget it," he repeated and looked at me with the grimace of a man misunderstood.

"Are you gonna go get Fantom or not?"

"What the fuck? Are you crazy? No! You're sick in the head!" he raved on, running his fingers through his hair. "Madness day in, day out, madness nonstop!"

"I get it," I said.

That didn't surprise me one bit, there in Susedgrad.

"Like hell you get it," he snarled, marched to the door, stepped out, and slammed it, making everything shake.

I stared at the door. His wife peered out of the room. She was holding a bald baby girl who was sucking at her breast. She immediately withdrew. "Where's he gone now?" she asked from the kid's room.

"To get Fantom," I said helplessly. Aware of how mad that sounded in Susedgrad.

Later she came back, buttoned up. As if she'd pulled herself together. I expected she'd rant and rave, but she decided to play along with it all.

"He'll be straight back," I said.

Finally she served the coffee. Perhaps breastfeeding is soothing, I thought. We tried to talk about something. Vital topics. I pretended to be mature and sensible. She was an economist by training and we talked about that a bit.

"The economy has potential . . . Until they catch you," I tried to quip.

"Oh really?" She raised her eyebrows.

The conversation stalled.

After a pause, I said, "So it's okay for you here?"

"Yeah, it's good."

We blew on our coffees and sipped quietly, burning our tongues. Danko was taking his time.

I waited for the door to open. She waited too, and she took on that ironic look again. We drank that coffee and spoke phrases that all meant "fuck it."

"I guess you've got a lot on your hands with the kid?" I asked.

We'd never met before, so I adopted an impersonal tone—it was hard to find the right way to relate to her. I thought of saying my name and reaching out my hand, but decided not to.

Danko was still taking his time. Probably half an hour had passed. A very difficult half hour.

We looked at each other over the table. She got up at last and made for the sink. She was fuming. With her back to me, I saw it in the way she held her shoulders and clattered the dishes. The water sputtered.

"Where is that loony?" she finally spoke through clenched teeth and turned around.

I shrugged. She went on washing up. Plate screeched against plate, and I shook. *Grrr*, she snarled.

I sat there. She washed all the dishes. She didn't have anything more to wash. She looked at me as if to say: What are you doing here?

"I don't know what now," I said.

"I don't know either." She came back to the table and took a cigarette from my pack.

"Help yourself," I mumbled.

She lit up and looked away somewhere. Certainly not at me.

I sat there and thought: you're condemned to this life.

Madness nonstop! It was Danko who said that. I said it too, and his wife as well. Their bald daughter still just suckled that madness.

You're condemned to this waiting, to this uneasiness, in all the places madness dwells. Ordinary, inexplicable domestic

ROBERT PERIŠIĆ

madness—plus me. In every house, always hidden in the dark of a room. It always whines there and only a mouthful of breast can quiet it. Breast, madness, madness, breast. Breast, madness!

I probably muttered that audibly.

"What?"

"Madness. That's all," I said.

She came right up close, stood in front of me, and slapped me. Madness in Susedgrad!

I stared at her. She took a step back and pointed to the door. As I looked at her, an indifference took hold of me. A clear thought came to me after my long wandering: there is no law. There simply isn't. And there is no God. It wouldn't be so bad if He existed, at least somewhere in reserve. But He doesn't. There is no law. She stood in front of me and showed me the door. What was the point of that? There was no point. What did I care? I'd show her the window.

I pointed at the window. And laughed, so what? There is no law. Now something pointless was bound to happen. Now even she started to laugh. She looked at me in disbelief. I accepted that, okay, I think it's funny too!

But she found it funnier and more absurd. There! She looked at me, raised her arms into the air, lowered them, and bent with laughter. I laughed too, but it was rather forced. Still, I couldn't stop smiling. It's better to laugh. Laughter brings people together who don't get on. It's funny when you realize it. She seemed to realize. *Ha, ha, ha!* She came up to me again and started beating me on the head. Hey, this woman is beating me on the head! I smiled stupidly, sitting there and not knowing what to do.

I was funny, I know, but okay, let her. Then she started to muss up my hair with both hands. As if I was her toy. She howled with laughter like an animal on a hill in the night. This is solitude, I thought, this is an explosion.

Her breasts were waving in front of my nose. *Hee, hee* she whinnied with all her lungs. It was good, let her explode! Those boobs dangled in front of my face and one of them bopped me on the nose. Through her shirt. And then again.

Shock, horror: I took hold of her waist, pulled her toward me, and started to bite her boobs through her shirt. Those boobs full of crazy milk. I fumbled and undid the buttons and started to suck. Suck, suck! Milk came out. My lips seized a large dark nipple, and then the other equally large nipple of the other boob, and then the nipple of the first huge boob again. Then she thrust me away. She went to the front door. I followed. She double locked it. Then she quickly pulled down her jeans and panties. She turned her butt to me and raised it with her hands. She turned back and looked at me with a plaintive grimace. We connected right away. Spot on.

We humped, deep and furious. She sank. Faltered. Fell. I caught her, held her boobs, milk was on my fingers, slippery. I put her back on her feet. She found her balance again. Visceral thoughts circulated in my head. No. Yes. Don't. Why not? She wants it. She does. She doesn't. No. No.

I pulled up my trousers and went to the table. I leaned against it with my arms. No. No, I thought . . . Dammit, it's too late.

I sat down. She squatted against the wall in the corner. She looked up as if she was gasping for air. Then she glanced at me. Her jeans were still down. She looked away again, stood up, and pulled up her jeans.

Later the phone rang.

"No, why should I be angry," she said.

"He is," she said.

"Okay," she said.

"Bye," she said. She turned toward me. "They're waitin' for you at the bar where you were before."

I got up and headed for the door.

"You know," she said, "don't come back again."

She frowned strangely, as if she didn't know why that came out.

When I opened the door, the kid started crying again.

I went down the stairs, and when I passed the door of the lady with the dog I was almost surprised they were still there. I heard shouting inside and the dog barking as if in a box.

I went out into the Susedgrad night, headed along a street that looked nothing like a main street; I walked, and walked, and finally came to something resembling a highway.

For Whom the Bell Tolls

"EVER SINCE I 'eard of the landlord, Aleksandar, there's been 'asslc with everythin' 'bout the apartment," I say to Ćmedo.

'E 'as no idea what I'm on about, an' says, "Who's that again?"

"The landlord, Aleksandar, meanin', y'know, the owner of the fuckin' apartment. They say like, 'e wcnt off to join the Chetniks, yeah, an' I moved into the apartment, what the 'ell. An', fuck, like, a few light years passed since then, an' I totally forgot about Aleksandar. Then I'm goin' up the elevator and this girl says to mc Alcksandar's been a rock-solid opponent of the system in Serbia the whole time, like, for 'uman rights. 'E's goodness in person, she says, and she saw 'im on CNN. 'E defends every-one, she says, you know, all the minorities: Serbs—rubbish, not Serbs, there it's Croatians—Albanians, 'Ungarians, Gyp-sies—rubbish, not Gypsies, there it's Croatians—y'know, an' says even, what's most important for 'er, that 'e also protects fuckin' animals, an', like, she's 'eard Aleksandar's comin' back to Zagreb for some tonguewag. An' what the fuck, the apart-ment belongs to 'im anyhow.

"Y'know," I say to Ćmedo. "Like, maybc 'c'll be wantin' to come 'ere to sleep."

And 'e, of course, 'as no idea what I'm on 'bout an' says, "Which girl d'you mean?"

"The girl in the elevator. Who fuckin' else? Are you even listenin' to what I'm sayin' or do you come 'ere with your brain turned off? The girl, y'know, in the elevator, she told me all of that, an' I looked at 'er . . . I mean, I'd looked at 'er before, she's spunky . . . But now I really stared. 'Ey, what are you gogglin' at? she asks, an' I zip out of the elevator. Now I peer thru the peephole as soon as I get 'ome, an' I kibitz nonstop, every two seconds, it sucks. It's a 'abit now. Paranoia, fuckin' 'ell. An' also y'know—an apartment full of whacky stuff, paranoia squared! Fuck, an' that on just over 400 square includin' the balcony. I'm tellin' you, I just stare thru the peephole. I'm glued to the freakin' peephole like I'm wearin' a monocle."

On top of that, everybody grins at me. An' when I told that to Ćmedo, you know what 'e says to me? 'E says with a laugh, "Yeah, Zero, you've always reminded me of what's-'is-name . . . you know, the spy in *Eye of the Needle*."

And y'know why I've got no peace anywhere now? It's a catastrophe, I can't chill at 'ome or outside either. When I'm at 'ome I stare into the peephole, an' when I'm out, like, I keep callin' myself. Get this: I call myself with my phone, y'know, to see if anybody's at 'ome. 'Cos, like, I've got a fixation on Alek comin' back, any moment like. Gawd, I'm a noodle, fuckin' 'ell.

Now I even started drinkin' in the apartment. Fuck, I sit down in the kitchen an' wait. I always buy twice the amount of beer 'cos I'm expectin' Alek to come join me. An' I think of what to tell 'im! I mean, fuck . . . I'll tell 'im everythin'! Every fuckin' thing, I mean, 'e's gotta be informed, ain't 'e?

An' so I've been sittin' in the kitchen for a month. So that when 'e comes we can shift to the livin' room, but I prefer the kitchen, like, it's 'omey atmosphere. Y'know, I never drink in

ROBERT PERIŠIĆ

the livin', though it's more comfy there, but, like, I just don't feel like boozin' as soon as I sit down on the couch, just sleepin'. An' I don't like to fuckin' wake up an' see all them cans on the linen chest Alek left. Talk about fuckin' awful taste!

I mean, just look at them shelves. It's like the Berlin Wall. And them ugly shades on the lamps, like somethin' you find on a hooker. An' the carpet with them colorful patterns, fuckin' Iranian origin, as if 'e bought it all to drive me round the bend.

Y'know, so I wait an' think to myself that I'll tell Aleksandar all about 'ow it started, 'ow it was, an' 'ow it fuckin' is now! I can 'ardly wait for 'im. I thought 'e was comin' last night, but 'e didn't. Who knows, maybe 'e'll come today.

First I'll surprise 'im, y'know, 'cos there's another fuckin' catch 'ere, it'll drive you round the bend. I'll tell 'im: This apartment of yours, I gotta tell you right off, I just used the space an' stared at them shelves an' shades, fuckin' 'ell, but I didn't screw nothin' up, really, nothin', okay, except for breakin' the washbasin. Everythin's still in good condition, y'know, but you're gonna 'ave problems, I gotta tell you, I think, I dunno. If I 'ad the title deed I'd sell the place.

That'll make 'is jaw drop, won't it, an' I'll tell 'im straight out, like: You know, while you were in Serbia fightin' for rights an' all, they built a church 'ere right next door, new an' enormous, an' it's all very nice, but guess what? When they ring them bells, like, in the mornin' around noon they ring for 'alf an hour at a stretch, an', fuckin' 'ell, it can make you wanna do somethin' kamikaze, I dunno. Fuck, they put in one 'ell of a sound system. Yep, all electric… Pure noise an' 'eavy metal. A pillow over your 'ead don't 'elp one bit.

And then, like, on the weekend when they 'ave mass… I come 'ome smashed an' everythin', with my belly churnin'… An' in the mornin'… it shakes me. Y'know, Alek, I got a fuckin' grenade launcher in the apartment, a trophy I brought back, an' I wanted to fire it at the bell. But fuck, 'ow can I when them speakers are all invisible, like God? Besides, y'know, I'm not a Chetnik, who'd "destroy religious buildings," like they say. An' I really am curious what you'll do when you move in.

An' when I turn up Zappa, like, you won't believe it: the neighbors call straightway 'cos of the noise. I mean, what are you gonna do with neighbors like that?

And, of course, 'e won't know what to say, 'ow to react.

Okay, I'll say to Aleksandar, no sweat, I turn down the stereo, later I go to bed, an' then I wake up in the mornin' with them bells in my 'ead, 'ungover like I am. An' the neighbors— nothin'…

I've called the cops a few times too, 'cos of the racket. I didn't know what else to do, but the cops, like—nothin'! They just took down my name an' looked at me like some freak.

"It's logical, y'know, whaddya expect," Ćmedo says to me. "The church gotta ring!"

"Why it gotta ring? Who's it ringin' for? I'm tellin' you, it's a custom from the fuckin' Middle Ages, like, when nobody 'ad a watch, so they 'ad no idea when it was time for mass, when it was six, when it was quittin' time, y'know, but today everybody's got a clock at 'ome. You just need to take a damn look."

It was kinda romantic, like, until they put in them electric bells. And now… Now, Alek, if you're such a big shot, you sleep 'ere, or at your place, whatever we're callin' it, I don't give a shit, just so I see 'ow long you can stand it for.

No, I'd really like to know if they've got some piece of paper, you know, legal permission, black on white, to ring 'em so loud. I mean, if you've got a pub an' the noise bothers the tenants, like, you don't just need a license but you gotta go to the tenants' association, you know, an' bribe 'em!

Okay then, so bribe me an' then ring! But fuckin' 'ell, I bet they ain't got no license!

'Ere, listen, they're startin'... I know, Mr. Aleksandar, that's why I'm tellin' you... An' I 'eard you fight for 'uman rights, that you protect Croatians an' everybody else too? So, fuck, I think you might be able to raise the issue, 'cos people 'ere won't—till Judgment Day... An' like I told you, if the apartment was mine I'd fuckin' well sell it!

A Former Poet Remembers

I DON'T KNOW what level you're at, but I took the placement test and realized I don't remember a thing from Advanced English.

A girl in wide trousers was sitting next to me. She glanced at me from time to time.

When she finished hers, she even said to me, "Ask."

She was so young.

"It's okay, ask," she said.

"No, I'll manage by myself," I muttered.

Then she handed in her test and left.

I was the last person to finish. Perhaps it was a kind of shock. As if only then I became aware how much time had passed. I'd unlearned everything.

No wonder, it was back when I was in Zadar. Sometime around 1988, '89. And I only remember meaningless things: the atmosphere, the way the light slanted into the classroom, Mr. Vuksan.

No, he wasn't a "mister" like people are in Croatia today— we had socialist nomenclature at the time—but he was "Mr." in our English-language classes. That's how we addressed each other in Advanced English.

Yes, Mr. Vuksan, an unforgettable character. A sad, drooping moustache, and always a gray suit. He spoke in a rush, with a very backcountry accent, in English, of course. We liked him. Despite his moustache he sat on a bench like a real school student, with a sharpened pencil. Whenever a question came his way he would hurry to field his own, as if he were fleeing before everything English. Maybe precisely because of him, everything began to resemble a real school. A ripple of laughter, which was not allowed, would run around the room.

It was hilarious: Mr. Vuksan compressed his English as if he was going to swallow it. We didn't even have to exchange glances. You know when it grabs you, like some form of telepathy. It's enough for someone to scratch their head. Someone else stares intently straight ahead. You communicate with incredibly small gestures, cheeks inflated, until someone bursts out laughing.

Mr. Vuksan didn't understand us and would look at the teacher. The Advanced English teacher was a bald gentleman with reading glasses. When the laughter burst out, he would raise his eyebrows. Those glasses and his high, furrowed brow . . . Huh, we're not children after all.

Who would have thought I'd remember Mr. Vuksan, of all people. I was probably eighteen at the time, and he—outmoded and gray, with a handlebar moustache—seemed to us the cliché of socialism.

I know, he felt uncomfortable stammering among us—young women and men of a new age.

Who knows why he enrolled and what it all meant for him? Why he paid for the course, and then missed a lecture for the first time halfway through the semester, because that day he jumped off a high-rise building.

Maybe he thought it would change his life, that Advanced English might be a solution, a new stage? But he didn't manage at all. The newspaper published his photograph in the obituary his mother wrote for him. I saw it.

"Look," I said at home. "This guy was with me in Advanced English."

My mother was surprised that people like that were in Advanced English with me.

Some others saw it in the paper too, and when we sat down in the classroom we didn't know who would say it. We only talked English in the class. I thought up the sentence, but someone said it, in a hollow-sounding tone. Telepathy. I don't know who did what. There was a split second of laughter, which was not allowed, and then silence. The teacher raised his eyebrows. I thought he would kind of put things right. But he didn't have anything to say except, "Well, it takes all sorts."

He said that, thinking of Mr. Vuksan. He said it in English. I forget how he said it. But I remember for sure that the feeling arose in me then. After he took our side, rather than Mr. Vuksan's, everything changed.

We went to a pizzeria after the class. I made sure not to be quiet, and I avoided eye contact with the others. As if I had begun to go into hiding, I went a few more times, and then I stopped.

You know, back then I had some fixations. I wrote poems and believed in secret I was a great poet. Perhaps that's why I became so emotionally involved. Because Mr. Vuksan was good for a poem.

Today I found that poem from Advanced English. It was dusty business.

I remember how it could have been at that time: late in the evening, a record on the turntable, me alone in the room, and I felt it was something for me—I needed to write a poem about that tragedy, as if it would allow me to compensate for what happened. People here look down on those who commit suicide, and I, as a lonely heroine of sorts, was on their side.

Later, when the new times came, everything from Advanced English lost significance, especially those pathos-filled poems about suicide, and my English was mothballed.

Can you imagine, Mr. Vuksan, how far I've dropped behind? For years I've only spoken Croatian, or nothing at all, and now something is pushing me to take Advanced English 11, as if it will change my life.

Strangers in the Night

WHEN WE CAME in New York, I don know, we was bit confused by everything. Where should we start? Such big town, you know.

And, you know, my friend Bađo, he very good person, but bit crazy, and, I don know, maybe bit stupid, lil bit, you know. So, we was first day in New York and, I don know, we walked and walked, and he asked everyone on street, "Tell me please, what is most dangerous place in New York?"

And everybody tell him Central Park, you know.

"That is very dangerous place at night. Don go at night!" said everyone.

And, I don know, I was thinking in my head, I wouldn't go at night, never, you know.

But Bađo was thinking deep and he tell me, "We must go to Central Park, tonight, my friend!"

I said, "O, no," you know.

But Bađo is thinking something else. He said, "O, yes, absolutely!"

"O, no, Bađo, it's me, you know."

"Completely yes!" said Bađo.

"Why?"

"We must go to see most dangerous place, because, after that, we will know everything, my friend," said Bađo.

I didn understand that philosophy, you know.

"Yes, my friend," Bađo said, "when we see most dangerous place, we will know what we could expect in all other places!"

"O, you think so?" I said.

"Yes. And we are free after that to go everywhere, in every place in New York, understand?" he said.

"But you know, it's most dangerous place," I said.

"Exactly! First we will see most dangerous place, and after that in all other places will be easy for us," said Bađo, bit crazy guy, you know.

And, I don know, we buy two cases of beer and we go sit in Central Park.

We sit there in twilight, five o'clock in afternoon, to wait in the night in Central Park, which is most dangerous place, you know.

But some people are still working, because it was nice day, you know. And, I don know, people looking at us quickly, and who knows what they are thinking in the head. They look at us and go other way, you know.

We drink beer, I don know, one, two, three, maybe, four beer, and darkness come.

It was very dark. We didn see anything, you know.

And, we are waiting. I don know, we waiting very long and nothing happen.

But, we wait again. And drink beer, you know.

In one moment, we heard voices and Bađo stand up and said loudly, "Who is there?"

No one answer, you know. Just silence came to us. I was bit scared. In this strange world, you know.

Bađo speak again, "Who is there? We are here!"

But no one answer. Just silence stay there and nothing move.

ROBERT PERIŠIĆ

And, I don know, we didn hear nothing, see nothing. Just drink beer and wait again in darkness.

We drink lot of beer and it become very boring, you know.

After one or two hour, maybe three, I don know, we heard voices again and we see cigarette light in dark.

Bađo stand up again and scream, "Hey you, come here!"

But no one answer and we didn see cigarette light anymore, you know.

Bađo is starting to lose his nerves, you know, and he scream again, "Come here, you motherfuckers! Come here to me!"

No one answer again.

And, I don know, Bađo lost his nerves completely and he couldn't stop screaming, "Come here you fucking mother-fuckers! Come here to me and my friend! Come, you fucking criminals!"

He was very disappointed, you know.

And, I don know, I start to scream with Bađo, "Come here, all of you! Come here, you fucking animals! Come here every fucking last all of you!"

But no one come, you know. Just deaf night, just big silence in dark wood in New York and, I don know, some kind of very bad feeling of loneliness, you know.

We wait and wait and drink beer and there was no one to see, no one to come, my friend.

And, I don know, after some time I realize Bađo and me starting to be very drunk, you know.

Bađo said to me, "This Central Park is nothing! It isn't dangerous place at all!"

I said, "Who knows!" I was very nervous, you know. When I am drunk and nervous I start to be bit dangerous, you know.

Bađo said, "Who said it's most dangerous place? This place is shit!"

But I wasn't so sure. I said to Bađo, "Maybe it's some kind of dangerous place, really."

You know, I realized we are some kind of dangerous people. And, we was in Central Park, you know. But it was impossible to explain to him. He couldn't realize, you know. He just couldn't!

He said, "What the fuck is this place? It seems we are most dangerous people here!"

And I said to him, "Maybe it's true." That was good moment to explain my idea, you know.

"It's fucking New York!" he screamed and looked in sky.

"Yes, it's fucking Central Park!" I was angry, too.

After we wait enough, finally I realize we are most dangerous people, really. I was thinking: who knows, maybe we are most dangerous people at all, you know. And, I don know, in some way, I become very sad about it. Maybe is no sense in this, but, I don know, I was feeling just like in some very sad story.

I said to Bađo, "Let's stop screaming, no one will come."

"Fucking criminals!" Bađo screamed. "Fucking Amerika! Why I come here? Why leave my beautiful country? Come here and tell me, you fucking motherfuckers!"

Bađo is my best friend, really. And I didn't know anybody else. I said, "I don know, Bađo, maybe we should move to some other place where is more light?"

Bađo stop screaming and look at me in dark.

"No," he said, "I will wait for them."

But, I don know, I was start to feel very strange in that wood in New York. I couldn't stay anymore, really.

I said, "Bađo, please, there is nothing here, let's go."

But Bađo answer nothing.

I wait in dark.

"Bađo, I will go along," I said.

I was waiting for answer, you know.

ROBERT PERIŠIĆ

"You can go," Bađo said.

"Yes, it's time to go," I agree.

And, I was walking along through dark wood and, I don know, I was bit sad and lonely. But, outside of this was big world waiting for me, you know. That was my hope.

And I go.

For *David Turashvili*

I Didn't Stop Drinking, But I Lost Hope

THERE WERE SEVERAL of us in the town. I mean, we who thought the same way all knew each other, of course. We were like a secret cell. Fanatics who would stop at nothing. An old professor, whom we titled The Doctor, was our ideologue. He taught Russian, English, and a lot of other subjects, depending what was required, and he had broad horizons. He was able to distinguish vodkas, not to mention beers and wines. We younger devotees weren't so good at that—we'd never had much choice—so we imbibed the Doctor's stories.

"I never stopped drinking, even under the most difficult circumstances," he said.

I can say that today, too, after all that's happened.

Booze flowed freely under the Russians. Those were liberal times there, at least that's what the Doctor told us.

It's not that nothing went on. There are those who look puritan and are closet drinkers. But the handful of us were hard-core, we were radicals and, whether you like it or not, word gets around. We drank more and more, perhaps as a form of protest, too. Since that's how we were, everyone knew we were pro-Western. Dissidents, as they say. Just for the record:

alcohol is officially prohibited there now, after all, in the regime the Americans helped establish. Democracy, like, but without alcohol. With the Russians it was different—it was the most "Western" system there.

You might laugh, but it was the most Western system, for women and in general.

You don't believe it? I see you know nothing about my country. Neither do the staff at the asylum agency.

See, the Americans first supported those who prohibit everything because they were against the Russians, you know. And why did they fight against the Russians? Because they're against the West. Because according to them there's no alcohol. Women belong in the home.

The Americans supported those who don't let you drink, just so as to prevent socialism. And it was, which was the main thing for them. But they neglected all the details. They left that to me.

You find it ridiculous, but when I look at all of that—I need to have a drink.

Because the Russians might have dealt with those who don't let you drink if it weren't for the Americans. Until the end of his life, The Doctor blamed the Americans for helping them take control. They were then so mad as to turn back the wheel just because we in the cities behaved differently.

You have to know something about my country, so let me explain. The Russians did not go there out of the blue. Domestic communists ruled before the Russians, but there were two factions that fought like cats and dogs for power, can you imagine? Domestic atheists, factions fighting over the details, and one of them invited in the Russians.

So there were a lot of people like me, liberals who drank. We weren't such a minority back then as we are today after all the years of persecution. If only they would grant us minority status now. But we don't even have that right. They could exterminate us and the UN wouldn't even notice. I mean, what sort of international community is that?

But okay, to cut a long story short, the Russians withdrew and those who ban everything won out, with the help of the Americans. The Americans didn't think what would come after. When some of those who don't let you drink became terrorists, that annoyed the Americans. So the Americans had to act again and deal with the terrorists who prohibited everything, because naturally there were no longer the Russians to deal with them, so now the Americans had to continue the communist Russian war against them. For me, the communists and the Russians and the Americans are all the West—I see it as the same war. You just have to look at things from my angle. Can you see all this? Don't you drink now. Of course I'm for the Americans. Or for the Russians, it's all the same. It's just that I remember the stuff about the Russians better from The Doctor's stories because I was a kid then—you realize that, I suppose.

So I and others similar to me welcomed the Americans as liberators, after all.

The Americans occupied us and we, of course, hoped it would at least be like under the Russians, if not better. I mean, for us who drink and our sympathizers. But the Americans had to deliver democracy, and also they didn't want to be seen to be interfering in our way of life. That was a major disappointment for us dissidents—we couldn't believe it would still be an offence to drink. You understand, don't you? It isn't the real West but a kind of democracy where you're not allowed to drink. That's how it is. And seeing all of that makes you drink, of course.

Okay, under the Americans it was actually easier to obtain booze, that was some improvement. Black-marketeering is pretty well developed, and if they catch you you'll manage to get out of it before you go to court. You sort it out somehow because, fortunately, corruption is also well developed.

I have the good fortune of coming from a rich family, and I have an education, as you can see. We who drink are the elite, that's just how it is.

But democratic rule has become shaky again, and the hills around my city are crawling once more with those who ban everything and carry out their agenda when darkness falls.

He who rules by day doesn't rule by night, you understand.

My brother is with them in the hills—my very own brother. That's what really devastated me. When I realized my younger brother had gone over to them I thought any further resistance was futile—things couldn't be put right anymore. It could have been, in the time of the Russians perhaps, but it's too late now. I didn't stop drinking, but I lost hope.

At any rate, my case had a history no one understands. I can't explain it to the people at the asylum agency. They don't grasp the historical context. Now I see you understand the reasons. And I see that I'll see my Ramses again.

You think I should speak without the historical context? Do you think that's possible? To just tell the ending? Hm, okay, you're the lawyer.

So I'll skip the story. It happened before I fled: my mother died after an agonizing few years with cancer, and you don't know if you're relieved that she's died and if you've had your fill of sorrow.

At the funeral I saw my younger brother who's taken to the hills and joined those who ban everything. People saw him, but no one wanted to report him, not only because they were afraid but also because his mother had died. Our father died years earlier—he stepped on a landmine in a village. He was a vet and one of the most highly educated people in the area. They'd gone there in a jeep, and he wanted to move away when he got out for a piss because there were women in the jeep, and he stepped into an unmarked minefield. He bled to death on the way to hospital.

Sorry, that was from before, but I had to tell it.

At our father's funeral my brother still looked up to me as a second father—he was only a boy—but now after our mother's funeral he and I sat in the house, and I kept thinking that I hadn't managed to bring him up and have a positive influence on him. But I was still the elder brother and I told myself I wasn't going to hide from him. When our sisters and their husbands left, I got out the whiskey and put it on the table, because it was my house and I needed a drink; mother was buried and, in a way, it was all over.

He watched me as I drank that whiskey, slowly, with water, and I said to him, "Well, here we are, alone together."

He looked at me with a hard face, scowled, and spoke the words, "You'll have to go."

That didn't surprise me all that much, but I asked why.

"You know very well," he said. "Word gets around. You hob-nobbed with the Americans, went to soldiers' bars, and maybe even did some spying—I don't think you did, but the others don't believe me—and we both know you were a bootlegger and sold the stuff to others."

"I sold it to friends. I don't get it for free, so I can't give it away," I explained.

I wanted to add: they sold it to me too. But then I realized it could create problems for someone.

"I'm telling you because I know what's in store for you: there are lists, and you're on one of them, and you're my brother," he said. "I told them: leave him as long as our mother's alive."

I saw he wore a heavy burden as he spoke those words. I also had a lump in my throat, and the sorrow for my mother returned. So I went up to him and put my arm on his shoulder.

"Okay, let's say farewell properly, for mother's sake."

We embraced and both began sobbing. Then we abruptly moved apart and sat down again.

He probably said what he did with the best of intentions because he knew I was a target, I thought as I sat there in my house, which I realized was no longer mine. Maybe I was an impediment to his reputation too, an embarrassment, so he wanted me to go. Otherwise he would have to sort me out himself, or even twist my neck, because they like it when things like that are looked after in the family. I don't know, to tell the truth, what he really thought and what he might have had to do. I reflected on that then, and I reflected on it on the road afterward.

"I have no choice but to drink this whiskey tonight, and then away, right?"

He looked at me and wanted to seem grim, but I had been the closest to him, my whole childhood he skipped along behind me, and now he was expelling me, and a shade of sadness, perhaps also a wince of shame, wavered in his eyes.

"Maybe you want to get rid of me so then everything will be yours," I said, to sting him.

"That's not true," he said, offended.

"How can I know that?" I said.

He raised his chin and looked at me with an air of superiority. Because I had put him so low.

"How will I know that when I'm gone?" I asked.

He reflected with a scowl and then said, "What's yours will still be yours. Let's give the house to the relatives and rent out the land. I don't need it now either. Have them send you half the money. We'll see who of us survives."

Right then I saw there was still some of my brother in him.

If father hadn't been killed, I think things would have been different with him. He was a lively boy, but he listened to me. Later he developed into a strong lad, with an excess of energy. He drank with me several times, and that made him even wilder. I didn't give him any more alcohol, although he wanted me to. I saw he wasn't mature.

I thought it would be best for him to marry, but I didn't look for a young woman for him. I thought he should choose one himself. But he didn't.

He became resentful of me, I later realized. He needed discipline and turned to those who offered order. Essentially, he only wanted to be good and straight.

If I didn't go he might still kill me, I thought.

If he could kill me, he'd probably have it easier with the others. But I didn't ask him about that. Since he wanted to be good and straight, I'm sure he was good at that too.

So you have a brother and you don't. That was my country. You have a brother and you don't. And he's good, and he kills me. Because if I were good, he wouldn't be. So the question here is which of us is good. But the question was resolved by the simple fact of him having a gun, and me not.

"Okay," I said.

He left into the night, and I drank the whiskey and smoked as I looked at my house from the inside and took my leave of everything in it. Then my tomcat—who had been asleep in the corner while we were speaking—came up and started to wind around my legs.

"Ramses, my friend, do you see all this. Do you see all of this, my friend?" I said to him. "What am I going to do with you, Ramses?

I stroked him and drank the whiskey in my former house, in silence.

Casanova of the Coast

IN THE MID 1980s I got a Tomos 14 motorbike with a sporty add-on exhaust—a really cool muffler that I bought from an unlicensed mechanic—because we wanted to soup up our bikes as best we could, and so, with that snazzy muffler chugging, I would ride from camp to camp without a helmet, with my long hair, knowing that the summer rushes by at the speed of light.

It all seems a bit incredible to me today: that sunken world, the outdoor bars and holiday camps, those Tomos bikes—the embodiment of our socialist system—that we farted around on, flirting with Western girls, and not feeling at all like we were losers. We had the advantage of being on our home turf: all those people came to our country, so it must have been good here, maybe even the best. If only I could get hold of a more impressive bike, I thought, there would be no limits; before too long I saw myself riding a black Yamaha, partly nickel-plated, like my older cousin who had a Suzuki 500 cc, a beast he earned by growing carnations in a greenhouse, which also demands hours and hours of work in a stooped position, so afterward it's entirely natural for you to hunch over a racing motorcycle.

In short, I believed in myself and in that prospect. We in Dalmatia generally don't have any great problems with self-confidence, that is, we're not meant to. My whole adolescence was played out in that tone—the tone of short statements: *So what? Who are you to tell me? That's my decision. I said so. Basta!*

I had to behave self-confidently like that, riding the bike, and when you behave that way you sort of slot into the role, you concentrate on your mission, you lose no time, you scan the scene with your bird's-eye view, maneuver along the coast like a gull in search of a shag, and home in. You wish you could make the summer a time machine, and every tourist girl is a UFO that you observe through your telescopes and establish that she's free, you approach in your spacecraft with that show-off muffler, and strike up a conversation in English, the language of the galaxy, and if that fails you switch to intergalactic pantomime—gesticulation. Admittedly, it didn't really work because words have always been important to me, although some of my friends managed to get something going even with women they couldn't talk with, which I must say is comforting.

We didn't view ourselves analytically, external impressions were more important for us, so we presented ourselves to each other as smooth operators, casually recounting deeds no one had witnessed because it's the kind of ground where there are no witnesses by definition, so people have to take your word. As men of the world, we had theories about what counted for Italian girls ("She has to fall in love a bit, and when she takes you by the hand you know you're almost there") and for German girls ("What counts is that she finds you sexy, and then you have a drink together"), so we knew everything. None of us was scared, we were still teenagers, and we collected those worldly names in our address books—Nathalie, Gloria, Lucia, Elke—like we once did soccer cards.

ROBERT PERIŠIĆ

We lived in a small, conservative society that held out unexpectedly well against the blows of modernity. Contact with different cultures and customs? Cipher. All of that remained *outside* and barely influenced our criteria on our home turf. Old mechanisms ran smoothly, the sphere of male-female relations was highly codified, town squares were the venue for exchanging meaningful glances and significant *not my type* affectations; there was really too much of that, which produced emotional roller-coasters and dramas, serious complications about where to look and how to behave, because everything was a sign: attractive girls walked like Cleopatras from old movies, everything was hyped and nothing usually happened. Everything was gridlocked on those squares and promenades—you were under scrutiny. It was a Mediterranean theater of gazes and glances, a codified stage, general surveillance, Foucault's *Panopticon*, *Waiting for Godot*.

We walked around on those timeworn pavements like Vladimir and Estragon.

Yes, you could walk, but essentially you had nowhere to go. And you can't look at the sea the whole time and admire it, like the continental types think who are irritatingly indoctrinated by touristic propaganda.

Oh, lucky you, they always said, which got severely on my nerves because, in a way, they were suggesting what poetic state I should live in. Oh, if they lived here, yes, they'd just look at the sea and everything would be great. They were actually suggesting what role I should play—the role of a child of nature, a native in metaphysical harmony with his environment, an authentic person to complement the picture postcards, a man of the sea beyond social definitions. Even today it warms the cockles of their heart to meet somebody ostensibly like that, and they talk about it in their big cities as if they've seen a Mediterranean bear.

It really is a peculiar thing to live in an advertisement, to grow up at the very source of those touristic images—the site of a myth that the propaganda attributes meanings to for consumers—to live in the Mediterranean as it once was, as the Croatia ad on CNN says. That can mean that a certain backwardness was expected here, because what is the Mediterranean as it once was if not endearingly backward, in a beautiful and sublime way.

I'm telling you, it was a real gridlock on those squares and promenades, with everyone constantly watching like surveillance cameras, but nothing ever happened. I zoomed around helter-skelter on that bike, a spin here, a spin there, as if I was trying to get away. The road seemed to be a way out. That's why those bikes meant so much to us—we were seeking a hole in space.

Since reality was occupied, the desire for mystification was great. Platonic attractions certainly existed. It was entirely normal to like a girl but not approach her for months. Since every move was a public act, an audience was watching everything and therefore you were nervous. It's one thing to be turned down in a big city, and another in a town. In a small town everything is bigger. Few things ever happen, obviously, so every trivial event resounds, it echoes in little stories and when you hash over things with friends, it echoes in your head, and you become constricted, a person the size of your town and society, and even if you know all of that it still affects you, you remain restricted, and when you get drunk and go for too much of a fling you become ridiculous, a weirdo, an outcast from reality on the road. The only ones who speak the truth in those towns are the outcasts. Truth is fundamentally ostracized in a small town.

Therefore you could easily hide that you liked someone. You didn't show it. You played a game for yourself and mystified things. Yes, some of us were secretly romantic, especially in the winter, inclined to eternal love and fantasies too idealistic to stand the test of practice, so those loves were endlessly being put off.

In the meantime you also daydreamed of a licentious, foreign summer, the way someone from a small town cinematically imagines life in a big city, except that here something big-city-ish came to us: young women who were different and freer. They came for their mythical summer vacation, which meant going out and having a good time, and they felt obliged to experience something; we awaited them here with our complexes, and we had a lot to make up for.

The clash of winter and summer mode caused some unexpected small dramas. No, it wasn't worth working under domestic conditions and getting sucked into that long-term structure, but I don't believe even a dormouse could hibernate so long that it would skip the spring; there was always time to fill. That distant year, I had a small drama: spring came, I bought that Tomos 14 in red, it wasn't registered yet, nor did I have a license. But who cares about the socialist police when you're on a bike and seeking a hole in reality? There was a girl, not very tall but so shapely and firm: we were one body when we went round the bends on my Tomos 14. There was nothing particular going on, just a flutter. I didn't "go" with her, we just rode around, and we found it kind of interesting, so we'd go on the occasional spin in the summer too; once we even fled from the police together by zipping into the alleys of the old town, where their Zastava couldn't go, and I seemed a real Butch Cassidy in her eyes. Truly, I don't know what I was thinking back then: it wasn't the first time I fled—whenever I saw a STOP baton I'd just keep riding, slipping away into side streets, or wherever, until one day. . .

But that's not important. What is: it was finally summer. A warm night on a sandy beach, and with me a pretty thing from Bosansko Grahovo, who I met just fifteen minutes earlier, when

Tandara and I sprang into action in the middle of the street with the question, "Sorry to bother, we're from the Party youth organization and doing a survey. What brings you two girls here, and what are the vibes like?"

That was our new style, a slightly parodic performance and, what else can you—a great accomplishment. Or so we thought, although there were also some misunderstandings with such blatant approaches. We laughed at ourselves when it flopped, but this time it worked.

Us two guys, the two of them, and things ran their usual course. It's hard to know how couples come together—something clicks, looks and smiles synchronize—but now Tandara wasn't overly satisfied because he ended up with the girl who wasn't exactly a looker, but she had a well-toned body instead and said she was into karate. She also had a shrill voice, an obtrusive irony from her hometown, and all in all she wasn't in favor of us splitting up into couples so suddenly.

He wasn't so hot about it either, but since my girl was in a different mood he was kind of obliged to keep watch, he didn't have much choice. True, he tried to get out of it at first by glancing at his new companion with a pained face, but when I scowled to send him as far away from me as possible he gradually disappeared into the darkness with the karate girl and tried to entertain her in some way—I could hear him—and he laughed at himself because of the nonsense he was spouting. Later, to my surprise, even she laughed.

But the conversation with my sexpot got bogged down when we entered secluded nooks of the beach and sat down, supposedly to gaze at the stars. The humor evaporated rapidly, we seemed not to be on the same wavelength, and the range of topics narrowed so drastically that we were even chatting about what our parents did. She said her father was a policeman. I

ROBERT PERIŠIĆ

hugged her nevertheless. Then I discovered her lovely breasts. At one point I raised my eyes a little and noticed a silhouette approaching us. I looked closely and saw . . . her! It was her—yes, her—not so tall but firm, my bike partner, walking barefoot over the wet sand down by the water. She scampered back from the waves that rolled up and touched her feet, and she hovered like a ballerina in a love scene. Now she came up very close, had a good look, and I hoarsely greeted her. She fluttered away just as she had come.

Something shook me there, although it didn't really hit me until the next day, because I realized I was in love with that bike partner. It's curious that I didn't fall in love until the next day, after she walked by in the street without even giving me a glance. Then, like the legends say, I saw what I'd lost. I could have sworn I'd lost the love of my life.

Okay, sometimes it's most convenient to fall in love when things are already in ruins so that you don't get caught up in it all really, and you still have some kind of emotional life.

Those impossible infatuations are curious in that they're like a simulation, an acting out of a big show for oneself, a staging of romantic disaster, because there's always a big obstacle in your way, or at least a stone in your shoe. Romantic love is hindered in too many cases, it has its own inherent justification and is often a pleasant way of being alone, of avoiding that whole profane world, the relations of supply and demand, while you wait for something big, wait for a miracle, because truly, sometimes it's better to wait. And to be safely away from people.

That was token infatuation—kind of phony—but it opened the door to bittersweet suffering.

In any event, the cute pillion girl now mistreated me, teasing me with hot and cold signs, while I took up position so she could see me sitting alone by the sea, staring into empty expanses, smoking Filter 160 next to my parked Tomos, waiting endlessly for her to come by and see that monodrama. And then I saw her one sad evening with a young German in a Hawaiian shirt, the next evening as well, and, to keep a long story short, he was the Kraut of her life; she chose the path of Western integration at an early age, and today she lives somewhere in Bavaria. And where should I go—to Grahovo to be the son-in-law of a cop?

No, that wasn't in the cards either, because in the meantime the Grahovo girl got in a huff.

Tandara, on the other hand, claimed I was indebted to him until his dying day after that unfortunate evening because at one point the karate girl had knocked him to the ground with a cunning grip, supposedly in front of passersby.

So traumatic moments followed for me in the days afterward with a chubby, partially deaf Swedish girl—I had to keep her busy while he was with her buddy, who was almost as attractive as the Grahovo girl. Pretty girls often go out together with unattractive ones, so Tandara and I exchanged those debts like in a barter economy. He was wingman for me, I for him, each of us was indebted to the other, and it was interesting to observe that we were actually more relaxed with those unattractive girls—you just needed to spend a few hours without ambition, chitchatting without slicking around and acting the Don Juan, and it often happened that the girl liked you. And if it you had to go out together two evenings in a row because he needed time with his chick, you'd have a right little pseudo-relationship. And, of course, instead of the hot one falling in love with him, the unattractive one fell in love with me, and after a time you didn't know what you wanted, you'd pretend you were just being silly, and she even eggs you on in all manner of ways, loses patience, throws herself at you in make-believe nonchalance. You withdraw, sit on the edge of the bench, everything is back

ROBERT PERIŠIĆ

to front, you're not a hotshot in the first place, but you become a good and bashful boy, and she especially likes ones like that, which she tells you in her partially deaf English. "I will love you and pet you and call you Daffy," they said to Bugs Bunny once, and to me many times.

I was sick of it! I wanted to be a slicker, not be chased around town by partially deaf Swedish girls. So that August I withdrew into the role of a lone wolf, a solo seducer. I went away on my red Tomos to a camp instead of into town, avoided Tandara, the Swedish girls, the police—all of that.

Of course, I knew a temp who worked at the camp reception desk. He was a friend too. I had lots of friends then, probably more than at any time later, because it was especially important for me in those years to have turbo friendships ("Hey bro, how's it doin'?" "What's new, hero?"), which made me a man instead of a random kid who didn't know anybody.

Frc, a slightly older guy, worked at the camp reception, so I settled into a reserve position and kept him company while he did his nightshift, as if I was employed there too, and we sat at the barrier and observed the comings and goings.

Apart from watching like that, there were also some less than legal ways of exploring the landscape. Frc simply let you look at people's papers at the reception, and you could sit there, flip through the pile of passports, look at photos, gaze at some for longer, slowly, like in a depressing Romanian movie about life in a police state. You noted what interests you on your piece of paper as if you were an interrogator from a touristic gulag: name, city, bungalow number. In the morning you got out the atlas and encyclopedia and looked up where that city is, which river flows through it, what kind of industry it has, what the local football club is called, what the culture is like, which composer was born there, and so on. Okay, I'm exaggerating a bit, but I took a potshot at an attractive French woman like that, knowing who she was and where she was from, and that she was twenty, and I devised what I considered a form of French, accentuating the books I'd read—not just French but also Russian ones.

Her name was Nathalie and she was studying psychology. She found me funny and constantly thumped me on the shoulder when we went out for drinks. We drank small beers all evening, then we kissed, it was going like a dream, and we arrived back at her bungalow arm in arm. We flopped onto the bed in the corner and, beneath the faint light from outside, I immediately started kissing her breasts, which in truth were smaller than the Grahovo girl's, but Nathalie was a beautiful brunette—I remember her as the Helena Bonham Carter type—and I soon managed to undress her, what's more, she assisted, it went so fast that it surprised me, because Nathalie was so free, lithe, avant-garde, her untanned breasts shone white in the darkness, and I kissed that firm body that writhed with anticipation beneath me, not just French but also Russian, it seemed, and I kissed and kissed, tasting her sweet sweat in my mouth, feeling her heat, smelling her sex in that sultry cabin, and I didn't stop, I didn't stop because I felt I had no erection, which stunned me, I thought it would grow but it didn't, so I said to myself—come on, come on—and all of that went on, and it became stifling in that damp chamber, and I didn't know what to do, how to withdraw from that disastrous event, while Nathalie panted—come on—and I started to remove my clothes, as if I was going to the axman's block, I stood in the darkness, climbed onto the bed, onto her, and saw that nothing had changed, then I kissed her again, although I didn't feel like it anymore, and my only thought was how to get out of there, how to vamoose, how to vanish from that utter debacle if it was possible; no, it was impossible, there was no way out, so

ROBERT PERIŠIĆ

I kissed, kissed and kissed her, and she tried something, and it all went on until she suddenly sighed, puffed through her lips on that bed in the corner, in that fug, and stopped.

She pulled the sheet over herself, leaned against the wall there, and lit a cigarette. She asked me if I often had that problem.

"No," I said.

"Only with me?"

"No... hm... Yes."

Then she said she didn't think I was terribly experienced, and I said no, and she said, "What do you mean no? Yes or no? Have you ever had sex before?"

"No," I muttered in the language of the galaxy, whose depths were sucking me into a dimension of no return, after total disaster.

Still, now that I'd admitted it she'd at least understand me, I thought.

"How old are you really?" she asked, and I told her—there was no escape—and she said, "Why did you lie?"

Why did I lie? Hm, that's so obvious, I thought, but Nathalie didn't wait for my reply.

"Oh Jesus, oh fuck!" as if it all hit her just now, and she told me, almost threateningly, to go immediately. "Please!"

That's not quite what I expected from her.

I hurriedly got dressed. I went to see Frc at the reception, with all of that in my head, as if I was lugging the whole bungalow with me, and I knew there was no way of expressing it all.

He asked with a knowing smile how it had been.

"Yeah... Good. Super," I said.

There was no way out.

"Did you fuck her?"

That was the usual way of asking.

"Aha."

I still had to lie, of course. The disaster was so dreadful, in my view, as to be unspeakable. Seen from my angle, I had found out most abruptly that something was wrong with me. I couldn't reflect on my mechanical approach, my sheer desire to appear as an adult, and the acting full of suppressed fear. I couldn't reflect on it all because I didn't know how it ought to look in the first place.

A man had to succeed. That was all I knew.

I was in shock. I had never heard of anything like this happening to anyone, and I asked myself if it was worth going on living.

I departed that horrible camp and zoomed away into that hideous night. I knew there was no one to talk with about this. A sham world stretched out before me.

Under My Shoe

WHAT DOES THAT say about the sanitary standards, we asked ourselves after one of us recounted that she had stepped on a mouse at the market.

"It just scuttled under my shoe—a tiny mouse."

"Did you squash it?"

"No, it ran off again, it wasn't hurt."

"Nooo, you just seriously injured it," we said as we laughed.

We should perhaps give some consideration to the sanitary standards at the market, where all kinds of things can end up under your shoe while you're checking if the fruit is ripe, and looking to see if it's artificial and imported, or real domestic produce.

The mouse stands crookedly in its hole. Now it hurts a bit, now it doesn't.

It just wanted to go on, ever and ever on, and don't tell me you don't understand.

ROBERT PERIŠIĆ was born in 1969 in Split, Croatia. In 1988 he moved to Zagreb, where he studied Croatian literature and became a freelance writer, penning literary criticism, poetry, plays, and fiction. His most widely translated works are the novels *Naš čovjek na terenu* (*Our Man in Iraq*) and *Područje bez signala* (*No-Signal Area*). But Perišić's reputation as a prose writer was established by his short stories. His collection *Užas i veliki troškovi* (*Horror and Huge Expenses*)—of which this is a revised edition—was received enthusiastically in Croatia and neighboring countries and was shortlisted for the *Jutarnji List* Award (which Perišić later won with the novel *Naš čovjek na terenu*), and it became thought of as one of the most representative books of the decade.

WILL FIRTH was born in 1965 in Newcastle, Australia. He studied German and Slavic languages in Canberra, Zagreb, and Moscow. Since 1991 he has been living in Berlin, where he works as a translator of literature and the humanities—from Russian, Macedonian, and all variants of the "language with many names," aka Serbo-Croatian. Between 2005 and 2007, he translated for the International Criminal Tribunal for the former Yugoslavia. Firth is a member of professional associations in Germany (VdÜ) and Britain (Translators Association). His best-received translations of recent years have been Aleksandar Gatalica's *The Great War*, Faruk Šehić's *Quiet Flows the Una*, Miloš Crnjanski's *A Novel of London*, and Robert Perišić's *Our Man in Iraq*.

willfirth.de

About Sandorf Passage

SANDORF PASSAGE publishes work that creates a prismatic perspective on what it means to live in a globalized world. It is a home to writing inspired by both conflict zones and the dangers of complacency. All Sandorf Passage titles share in common how the biggest and most important ideas are best explored in the most personal and intimate of spaces.